I0683374

FLATHEADS

BYRON STARR

FLATHEADS
BYRON STARR

Flatheads is part of cgp's chapbook collection.
Flatheads is also available as an ebook.

CGP-2009
ISBN 1-894953-08-8
ISBN-13 978-1-894953-08-5
Chapbook edition
©2002 Byron Starr – All rights reserved
Second printing, October 2010
©2010 Byron Starr

Cover art by KLD ©2003

Published in Canada by Creative Guy Publishing

FLATHEADS
BYRON STARR

creative guy publishing
vancouver | canada

A Logger's Lexicon (or loggin' jargon)

Here are a few of the terms used by the common logger in East Texas. This mini-glossary is by no means required reading for **Flatheads**. In fact, with the exception of the title itself, I tried to shy away from most of the logging industry's lingo for fear it would clutter the story. However, this brief glimpse into the language of the loggers should provide some insight into this unique trade.

Bed a tree, to. To level up a path in which a tree is to fall, so that it may not be shattered.

Binder chain. A chain used to bind a load of logs together.

Bird Beak. When felling a tree, a wedge cut into the trunk.

Board foot. A unit of measurement equal to 12 by 12 inches and 1 inch thick.

Bunk load. A load of logs not over one log deep.

Butt cut. The first log above the stump.

Catface. A partially healed fire scar in the stem of a tree.

Chaps. Protective leggings worn by sawhands.

Chock Block. A small wedge to prevent logs from rolling.

Choker. A noose of wire rope by which a log is dragged.

Choker hook. A hook fastened to one end of the choker.

Cross-cut saw. A saw which cuts the wood fibers on the cross section.

Cruise. To estimate the value of standing timber.

Cull. Logs which are rejected, or parts of logs deducted in measurement on account of defects.

Dogleg. An abnormal curve in the trunk of a tree.

Grab skipper. A short iron pry or hammer, used to remove the skidding tongs from a log.

Hang up. (1) To fell a tree so that it catches another instead of falling to the ground. (2) To get a saw stuck in the truck of a tree.

Haul. The distance and route in which the logs must travel.

Landing. A place where the logs are hauled or skidded before they are loaded.

Loader. A power loading device used to load logs onto a truck or railcar.

Logger. One who is engaged in logging.

Low boy. A flatbed trailer for hauling heavy equipment.

Mill Pond. A pond near a sawmill in which logs to be sawn are held.

Notch. To undercut a tree in preparatory to felling it.

Overcut. To cut above the estimated timber value.

Pig tail. An iron device driven into trees or stumps to support a wire or small rope.

Pine Sawyer. A beetle which attacks the sapwood of pine logs.

Pin worm holes. Small holes in timber and lumber made by the larvae of certain beetles.

Ring rot. Decay in a log, which follows the annual rings more or less closely.

Sap Stain. Discoloration of sapwood.

Saw timber. Logs suitable in size for logging.

Sawhand/Sawyer/Flathead. One who fells trees. Chainsaw operator.

Scaler. Person who determines volume of logs in a load.

Shotgun. To aim a tree in felling it.

Skid. To drag trees from the stump to the landing or mill.

Skidder. A heavy vehicle used to skid, or drag, logs from the stump to the landing or mill.

Skidding chain. A heavy chain used in skidding logs.

Skidder trail. A beaten path along which a skidder regularly travels.

Sound knot. A knot in a tree that is solid across its face, as hard as the surrounding wood, and so fixed that it will retain its place in the piece.

Spur. A branch logging railroad.

Swell butted. As applied to a tree, greatly enlarged at the base.

Throw. (1) To topple over with wedges a tree that is being felled. (2) to drop a tree in a particular direction

Tong. To handle logs with skidding tongs.

Top. To cut the top out of a tree.

Undercut. To cut an amount below the estimated timber value.

Waste. The portion of a tree which has merchantable value, but is not utilized.

Widow maker. (1) a broken limb hanging loose in the top of a tree, which may fall and cause serious injure to a man below. (2) A tree which, in falling, has lodged into another tree rather than falling to the ground. (3) a breaking cable.

Yard. *See* Landing.

L　　A　　T　　H　　E　　A　　D　　S

—One—

DAWN'S FIRST RAYS had yet to reach the tops of the tall pines, but if a giant scythe were to level all the trees in the east it would be evident that the sun had just risen and was currently making its slow ascent to this side of the globe.

The East Texas woods were quiet on that hot July morning. It was not the peaceful quiet of a few scattered songbirds and a few dozen late-morning crickets; it was a strange dead silence that was only broken by the whistling of the wind as it passed through the trees.

Slowly, a light rumbling grew in the distance. As it drew closer, the sound intermingled with the whisper of the wind, then it slowly replaced the wind, becoming the only sound that could be heard throughout the woods. The rumbling grew until it became clear that the origin of this sound could be nothing other than one of the battered log trucks that were so common to this part of Texas. Soon the sound made a dramatic increase in both volume and pitch as the truck geared down to climb a particularly steep hill. The auditory evidence of the truck's presence was then joined by visual proof, as twin pillars of black smoke rose from the other side of a hill down the road.

However, the log truck wasn't the first vehicle to come into view. A smaller vehicle first poked its head over the hill. It was a four wheel drive extended cab pickup, whose faded light blue paint was only visible in a few random places that weren't covered in dust, mud, or grease. It was readily apparent to all that *this* was a work truck.

Next, the log truck crested the hill, still belting out its high note and billowing a pair of smoke-plumes from its stacks. The truck's cab was similar to that of the pickup in that it was covered with dust, mud and grease; under all that grime, the log truck was actually white, but it would take a close look indeed to tell.

The reason for the truck's difficulty in climbing the semi-steep hill wasn't a heavy load of logs, instead, the truck was carrying a low flatbed trailer loaded with a skidder and a bulldozer, both of which were just as grimy as the log truck and pickup.

The peculiar silence of the woods was lost on the five occupants of the pickup.

* * *

In the center of the front seat, Kevin Harvey stretched his mouth wide in a yawn.

The big man behind the wheel of the pickup caught sight of this and grinned. "I thought you said you was used to getting up this early."

"Is he yawnin', Mack?" Roy Laviolette, one of the two men in the back seat of the extended cab, asked with a grin.

"Sure is," Mack replied, "Never known a man to open his mouth that wide. Seen a gal or two do it, but never a man."

This brought a brief round of laughter from the pickup's occupants.

"You sure you don't want any coffee?" Harry Gregg asked from the backseat as he held up an ancient-looking steel thermos.

Kevin finished his yawn and replied, "No thanks."

"That's okay," Mack said; then he affectionately slapped his big hand on Kevin's knee. "I'm sure on the same day you wake up and find you've got hair on your chest and your balls have dropped, you'll develop a strong likin' for coffee."

More laughter erupted from the back seat of the truck.

Kevin took the good-natured teasing in stride. Being the new man on the crew, he'd expected as much.

Kevin wasn't just the new man on the crew; he was new to logging altogether. Like most college students, he always returned home for the summer and got a job that would put a little money in his pockets. He had always earned his summertime spending money by sacking groceries at a local grocery store, but this summer he found that the job had grown stale on him. It had never been what he would have described as exhilarating, but this summer he found it absolutely unbearable. He hadn't been out of college and back at the grocery store for a week before he was looking for a new line of work. It was while tossing back a few beers with an old friend that Kevin had come up with the logging idea. Derek Monroe had graduated high school with Kevin and had always been one of Kevin's closest friends. Like many country boys, Derek had lacked the money to go to college and had started to work right out of high school. He had been on Mack Barton's logging crew for three years now and had been right in the middle of telling Kevin a typical *cut trees from sunup till late-thirty then drink beer and shoot the bull until dark* story when he saw his friend's eyes light up. Derek had tried to talk Kevin out of his crazy idea to take up logging for the summer, but he found his friend quite insistent.

Seeing that his efforts to talk some sense into Kevin were coming to naught, Derek took Kevin out and taught him what little he could about the job. Kevin's entire training had consisted of illegally sawing and debranching a solitary tree in the national forest. Derek then asked Mack about taking Kevin on as a sawhand. Even though Derek attempted to pass Kevin off as being *somewhat unskilled*, it had taken no small amount of persuasion for Derek to talk Mack into hiring a new man. But in the end, good old Mack had come through and even allowed Kevin to borrow some of his older equipment— including the much-needed chainsaw.

"How did we get screwed into starting this job on a Friday?" Derek asked from his seat by the passenger's door.

"The owner of the tract couldn't go out and meet me until yesterday." Mack grumbled, "I told him that we'd rather start next Monday, but he's in some kind of hurry to get his money for those trees."

"What's wrong with starting the job on a Friday?" Kevin asked, thankful to have the subject changed to something that didn't pertain to him.

"Bad luck," Roy offered from the back seat.

"Yeah," Mack seconded, "You start a job on a Friday, and it never fails; shit breaks down left and right, and about half the time someone ends up getting hurt. I never start a job on Friday when I can get around it."

"I wouldn't have placed you as the superstitious type." Kevin said to Mack.

"Son, let me tell you," Mack said, wagging a thick finger for emphasis, "You work around chainsaws and falling trees long enough, you'll develop a little superstition. I'm tellin' you, loggers are strange folk. I know one contractor who would turn down a job if there was a cemetery neighboring the tract."

"Jerrod Haskins," Roy injected.

"That's him," Mack acknowledged; then he jabbed a thumb toward the back seat and said, "Hell, ol' Roy has one of the weirdest rituals of them all."

"What's that?" Kevin asked.

"From the time we start a job until the job is done, he never brushes his teeth."

"Never?" Kevin asked in a somewhat subdued voice.

Behind him, Roy had taken out his false teeth and was creeping them over Kevin's shoulder. Suddenly, he thrust them into Kevin's face and said, "Yep, just soak 'em."

The sudden appearance of Roy's teeth made Kevin almost jump into Derek's lap.

Laughter roared through the pickup to the point that Mack almost had to pull over to keep from having an accident.

The laughter had just tapered off when the pickup passed over a small bridge that was little more than a culvert and guardrails.

"There it is," Mack said, pointing at a path in the trees that was just a hundred yards or so past the bridge. It was a clearly visible path into the woods that was nevertheless marked with a pair of orange ribbons tied around trees on either side.

"Looks like a good road," Roy commented.

"Yeah, it just needs a little widenin' and it'll be fine," Mack said.

The pickup pulled off the road and into the ditch, and the log truck pulled off right behind. Everybody piled out of the pickup, and got to work on unloading the dozer and the skidder. After all the tie-downs had been removed, Mack backed the dozer off the flatbed, and parked it near the edge of the woods.

Still sitting in the dozer's seat, Mack lit up a fat cigar.

Next came the skidder. Roy, the crew's skidder driver, climbed in the machine's cab and fired up its loud diesel engine. The skidder was a machine built especially for the logging industry. Its four massive four-foot tall tires were made especially for off road driving, enabling it to go almost anywhere. Its purpose was to drag the logs from where they were felled and debranched to a central location, where the crane operator would load the logs onto a trailer for delivery.

Once the skidder was off the trailer, Mack motioned for Roy, who climbed down from the skidder's cab and walked over to where Mack was sitting on the dozer's tracks puffing his cigar.

"Roy, I want you to keep an eye on that new kid," Mack said. "Derek said he's a little wet behind the ears, but I don't think the boy's ever picked up a saw."

"You want me to stick Harry with him for the first couple shifts?" Roy asked.

Mack thought this over then replied, "Naw, make the boy earn his dollar. Just keep an ear open for him before you start up. If it sounds like he's doing okay just drop by and check on him a couple times. Hell, we can't hold up the entire operation 'cause of one green flathead. Tell Don to go ahead and get the loader and bring Robert; by the time they get back I should have the path widened. Ya'll go ahead and get down there and get to work. The road dead-ends about a mile and a half into the woods, that's where our tract is. It's marked with orange ribbon."

"All right," Roy said, and he started back toward the log truck.

At the truck, Roy gave Don his instructions. As soon as Don had turned his truck around and started back for the loader, Roy walked over to the pickup where Derek, Kevin, and Harry stood waiting.

"All right, ya'll load up, and follow me down." With that, Roy turned and walked toward the skidder while the other three men climbed into the pickup.

* * *

After driving well over five miles into the woods, the skidder stopped, and Roy stuck his head out of the window and motioned for Harry to do the same.

"What?" Harry called out from the driver's seat.

"Have you seen any ribbon?" Roy yelled over the skidder's noisy engine.

"No, but didn't Mack say it'd be at the end of this road?"

"He said the road was only a mile and a half."

Harry shrugged.

Without another word, Roy climbed back into his seat and the skidder continued back down the trail with the pickup following close behind. They made their way slowly down the path for another two miles before the road abruptly stopped. Orange flagging could be seen wrapped around the trees where the trail played out.

Harry, Kevin and Derek climbed out of the pickup and started checking over their equipment and sharpening their chains, while Roy got out of the skidder and walked over to have a look at the flagging. Roy didn't consciously notice the strange silence of the surrounding woods, but he could tell something just wasn't right. He walked up to the line of ribbons and glanced at the trees they were to cut down. They were huge, most of them over one hundred feet, and a few possibly as tall as one hundred and fifty feet.

"Ya'll better change your bars," Roy called over his shoulder, "It looks like you're going to need twenty-eight inchers today."

Then Roy noticed something odd about one of the orange ribbons. He remembered that Mack had said the land was surveyed only a week ago, but it certainly looked like it had been longer than that—much longer. The orange ribbon had been swallowed up by the tree in several places, as if the tree had grown several years since the ribbon was last tied around its trunk. Roy walked to the next ribboned tree and found it wasn't quite as bad; it only had one side partially covered. But when Roy stepped off the distance to the next tree, he found that it was even worse than the first; the only evidence of the ribbon's existence was a circular scar around the tree's trunk where the tree had grown over it completely. Roy stepped to the next tree. At first he thought there was nothing strange about it, then he realized how loose the ribbon was. If it wasn't for a limb directly beneath where the ribbon had been tied, the ribbon would have fallen all the way to the ground. It seemed as if this tree had shrunk.

"Hey, Harry." Roy called out, "Come look at this."

Harry put his saw down, and made his way over to where Roy was standing.

"Look," Roy said, pointing at one of the ribbons that was almost swallowed up by the tree.

Harry glanced at the ribbon, and commented, "Looks like this place ain't been surveyed in a long time."

"The ribbon don't look old though," Roy said.

"It's old enough to have a tree growed up around it."

"But it's not faded. It's still bright orange. And not all the ribbons are like this. Some look good as new," Roy said, deciding at the last moment to leave off the part about it looking like some of the trees had shrunk, because it sounded a little on the ridiculous side.

"Maybe some're from an old survey and some're from last week," Harry said with a shrug.

"Then how come the ribbons are all the same color, and why aren't the older ones faded?"

"Hell, I don't know," Harry replied. "Maybe it was surveyed by the same company and they use some sort of new ribbon that don't fade."

Ignoring Harry's lame explanation, Roy simply shook his head and said, "I just don't like it. Something ain't right."

"You sure are lettin' that Friday thing eat at you," Harry said.

"It ain't that."

"Then what?"

Roy paused. "Nothin', I guess."

Harry chuckled. "If you ask me, I think you had one too many cups of that mud you call coffee. Next week, I'm making the coffee." With that, Harry turned and walked back to the pickup.

Roy stayed behind for a little while longer, staring at one of the half swallowed orange ribbons. It made Roy feel somewhat uneasy, but he knew that there had to be some sort of a logical explanation. There just had to be.

After taking one last look at the ribbon, Roy turned and followed Harry back over to the pickup.

* * *

With Derek and Kevin sitting on the pickup's tailgate, Harry sitting on a cooler, and Roy propped up against the skidder, the four of them shot the bull and made their final preparations before they went out. Nowhere was the difference between Kevin and the other men of the crew more apparent than in their appearance. Kevin's borrowed equipment was much the same—chainsaw with a twenty-eight inch blade, protective leather chaps, yellow hardhat, safety glasses, and gas can. But Kevin still appeared noticeably different. For one thing, Kevin looked conspicuously clean. Harry and Roy, and even Derek to a lesser extent had a sort of permanent grimy look to them. Not that they were filthy or unclean people—although Harry came fairly close—it was just that several years of working outdoors, as well as working on the logging equipment, had given them permanent dirt and grease stains under their nails and hard calluses on their hands. Their work clothes were adorned with tears and stains, badges of honor from several years in the woods—this was in stark contrast to Kevin's clean blue jeans and tee-shirt. The three experienced loggers also looked darker than Kevin. Derek and Roy could thank their Cajun bloodline for their dark complexion, but even Harry, who was a typical American mutt, was two or three shades darker than Kevin. There was no doubt Kevin would have a burn on his arms and the back of his neck by the end of the day.

After a couple more minutes, Roy decided it was time to get to work. "All right, we'll meet back here at, say, eight o'clock. That'll give ya'll just under two hours of cutting before the first break. Derek, you go to the left, and Harry you take the right. Kevin, I want you to go straight ahead about fifty yards and start there. You're the new flathead here, so I'll drop in and check on you every now and then." Roy turned and walked to the skidder.

Derek had started into the woods to the left as soon as Roy had given him his direction, but Kevin, weighted down by his stirrups and equipment, ran as best he could to catch up with him. "Hey, Derek." Kevin called out, making his friend stop and turn around. "What's a flathead?"

"A sawhand," Derek said with a smile, then he gave Kevin a rap on the top of his hardhat, "'cause we're the ones that end up with trees fallin' on our heads."

"Very funny," Kevin said dryly, beginning to feel a teensy bit nervous.

"I believe you're supposed to be cutting over there," Derek said with a grin, pointing in the direction Roy had directed Kevin to go.

Kevin turned and started off into the woods. Behind him he heard Derek's parting words of advice, "Don't forget, respect your saw; if you're not afraid, you need to get out of the woods."

—Two—

AS DEREK WALKED through the woods, he couldn't help but notice the strange silence. He stopped, set his saw down, and listened closely while he had a look around. Aside from the soft whisper of the wind, there were no sounds in the woods, and Derek's eyes found no sign of any other life other than the trees. And what monstrous trees they were. Rising straight and tall like monstrous wooden spires, they were impressive, and maybe even a little intimidating.

Derek looked one particularly tall pine from the bottom all the way to the top. His gaze reached the top of the tree, with his head tilted back and his mouth wide open. His hardhat toppled from his head to the ground behind him.

Gazing upward, Derek noticed that there weren't even any birds flying over.

Behind him, Derek heard a chainsaw buzzing and figured that the time for sightseeing had come and gone. It was time to get to work. He picked his saw back up, placed the gas can near the base of a tree so it wouldn't get run over by the skidder, then he walked over to the tall tree that had captured his attention. After finding a lane clear of other trees in which to drop the massive pine, he fired up his saw. Pulling the trigger, he received satisfactory rip from the engine; the steel teeth blurred along the twenty-eight inch bar. Derek made his first cut on the side of the tree that faced the direction he wanted to throw it. He then made another cut that ran down into the first, making a large wedge in the tree's trunk. After removing the wedge, Derek briefly rechecked his lane, then he positioned his sawblade against the back of the tree, where he wanted his third and final cut.

Derek squeezed the trigger and started his cut. The saw buzzed loudly, alternating its sounds from a fast buzz to a deep growl as Derek cut through the back of the tree toward the wedge. Wood chips flew from the tree, as the saw cut deeper and deeper. Finally, a loud popping noise sounded from within the tree, then another. Derek removed his blade, and stepped back. There was a series of loud pops as the tree descended, and a muffled crash when the tree hit the ground.

Derek smiled as he looked down the length of the tree. This was by far the largest he'd ever taken down, and it wasn't even the largest in the immediate area. Derek always got a bit of a thrill from dropping one of the big ones. He imagined a city-bred environmentalist might consider this a bit morbid, but it was nothing more than taking pride in his job. Like Mack always said, *let those damn tree-huggers wipe their ass on a plastic product and see if they don't develop a little respect for the logging industry.*

Next came debranching. Derek walked his way up the length of the fallen tree, taking off all the branches one at a time. When he was finished, Derek cut the tree's trunk into sections that could be dragged by the skidder, then loaded onto a log truck for transportation.

Finished with his first tree, Derek started on another one, then another, then another. Soon he had dropped eleven of the massive pines and was drenched in sweat for his efforts.

He paused to take a drink of water from a canteen he carried slung on his back; when he did, he noticed something strange. The tree he had just cut down was in plain sight, but where was the one before it? Surely Roy hadn't come up and dragged it off without him noticing. Derek set his saw down, and walked back to his last tree. He looked around the area, but saw no tree, not even a stump. What was even stranger, Derek was sure that a tree he saw standing was the one he had cut down.

He walked back down the area he'd been cutting, counting the stumps as he went. There were only seven stumps. But that was impossible, he knew he'd cut more than that.

He recounted, but again only came up with seven stumps.

A chill ran down his spine.

A chainsaw buzzed in the distance.

Derek looked at his watch, *7:43.* Just a little over fifteen minutes until the first break.

He *had* to have miscounted, there was simply no other explanation. Trees just don't get back up after they've been taken down.

He slowly walked over to another tree, and prepared to make another cut. As he did, he made frequent glances over his shoulder, half expecting to see a tree slowly and silently rising up from the ground.

* * *

Harry spit a black stream of snuff and smiled as his sixth tree crashed to the ground. He couldn't get over the size of the trees in this area; they were monsters.

As Harry debranched the fallen pine, he stepped over a small stream that the tree had fallen over. Harry paid no real attention to this little stream on his way up the length of the tree, but as he was on his way back down he stopped and gave the stream a closer look. Hadn't it been running the other direction just a second ago? Harry dismissed this thought almost as soon as it passed through his mind. Of course not, that's impossible.

Harry shook his head and walked on.

Behind him he heard the skidder. He turned and saw Roy in the process of lowering the big machine's rear claw to another log.

Harry found another tree, and got started immediately. After he found his lane, he cut a deep wedge in it, then he made the final cut and watched the tree fall.

He set down his saw, and stood up on the stump to get another good look at the tree before he started debranching.

As Harry stepped down from the stump, he noticed something peculiar. He kneeled down beside the stump for a closer look. Upon closer inspection, the stump went from peculiar to downright weird. There were no rings in the tree. All trees have rings inside their trunks that mark each year's growth, but this stump appeared to be one solid beige color, from the outer bark to the center of the tree.

Harry stood up and walked back to one of his earlier stumps, and, sure enough, these stumps were the same. They were solid through and through with no rings at all.

Not only that, but Harry only found five stumps. He was positive he had cut down six.

Harry spit a steam of snuff on the ground and muttered, "I must be losin' it."

Not far away, Harry could see the skidder picking up another log.

Harry waved.

* * *

L   A   T   H   E   A   D   S

The skidder had started acting up almost as soon as Roy started hauling logs. It died three times before he could get it rolling, then the engine quit once more before he could pick up his first log. On the way back it died once more and sputtered like it wanted to shut down a third time. Roy knew this skidder as well as he knew his own wife, probably even better. He had just completely rebuilt the motor last month and had thoroughly checked everything out before loading her onto the flatbed this morning. There was no explanation for this strange mechanical behavior.

Once the first log was placed near the road where the loader could easily get to it, Roy got back out of the cab and looked around. The skidder was purring like a kitten—well, maybe an eighteen-ton metal kitten, but it sounded like nothing was wrong with its engine.

Friday, Roy thought, shaking his head.

He climbed back in the cab and had a seat. Almost as if that was its cue, the skidder started sputtering. He pressed the accelerator, causing the huge lazy kitten to roar briefly, but as soon as he let off, the sputtering started once again, then the engine died with a shudder.

"Damn it!" Roy swore, taking his baseball cap from his head and throwing it into the controls. It smacked the steering wheel and fell into the floorboard, where Roy left it.

Roy turned the ignition key and was somewhat surprised when the engine instantly roared to life. He sat in the cab for a few minutes, trying the throttle out at different RPMs and listening for any sounds to come from the engine that could let him know what was wrong. Nothing. Everything seemed to be working fine. He scratched his semi-bald head in confusion. He revved the engine once more, just to be sure; it sounded fine.

After retrieving his cap from the floor and placing it on his head, Roy slipped the skidder into gear and started back toward where Harry was cutting. The big machine cruised along the path that had been made in the brush by the log it had just dragged into place. Once along the return trip, the engine shuddered, but it never came close to dying.

Roy drove up to his second log and tried to lower the crane to pick it up, but found the controls wouldn't cooperate.

"Oh, come on!" he swore and was just about to fling his hat again, when the controls suddenly decided to cooperate and drop the claw hard onto the log. No damage was done, but the sudden jolt that had rocked the skidder's cab caused his heart to pound away like a hammer in his chest.

Roy maneuvered the claw onto the log, and was about to turn about and start back when he saw Harry standing at the edge of the woods. It seemed that Harry was just standing around, not doing a thing. Harry wasn't exactly the best sawhand that had graced the pineywoods of East Texas, but he was no slouch. It wasn't like him to stand around idly when there was work to be done.

Harry waved.

Roy opened the door to the cab and hung his head out, "What's up?"

Harry looked around him for a second, then took his hard hat off and wiped his brow. It looked like there was a serious debate going on in Harry's head as to what to say. After another nervous glance around him, the debate was decided. "Uh, nuthin'."

Roy was a little confused by Harry's strange behavior. He called out, "You sure?"

"Yeah," Harry said, sounding about half like he meant it this time. Harry picked up his saw, and started for another tree.

Roy started back with only his second log of the day. The skidder died twice on the return trip.

* * *

While Roy was having a hard time with the skidder, Mack was having no problems at all with the dozer. In fact, the road was already almost wide enough for the trucks as it was. The only problem was, the road seemed much longer than it had been. Not only that, but the further in the woods Mack went, the more he was shocked by the immense size of the pine trees; he was positive he would have remembered seeing trees this size. In fact, if he had seen trees like this when he'd looked the tract over yesterday, dollar signs would have immediately popped up in his eyes.

Mack pushed a clump of brush and dirt to one side of the road, backed up, and started forward again. With the road as good as it was, he was simply driving down much of the road with his blade up. Every now and then he would stop and push a bit of dirt or an old log to the side, but not much more than this.

Mack stopped the dozer, killed the engine, and looked around. The dozer had no odometer, but he was good at judging distances. He figured he had already driven almost three miles, twice the length he thought the road had been yesterday, and he could only faintly hear the saws buzzing ahead. He began to wonder if they'd taken a wrong road. No, that was impossible, he had marked the road himself. He remembered the small bridge and the creek that ran under it. He remembered the two old houses before the creek. There was simply no doubt that this had to be the place. Maybe he wasn't remembering it correctly, because he'd had a nip, or rather a pint, of vodka before he went out to check out the tract. It wouldn't be the first time he'd made a mistake due to liquor, and he was certain it wouldn't be his last.

Mack looked at his watch, *7:45 a.m.*

He almost choked on his puff of cigar when he saw this. Surely he hadn't been out here piddling on the dozer for an hour and forty-five minutes.

The engine gurgled and sputtered as Mack tried to fire it up. When he finally did get it to start, it sputtered a few times and died.

"Damn!" he swore aloud.

This just wasn't right at all; he'd always said that in over thirty years in the logging business he'd found only two things he could truly rely on and they were Roy and his old dozer—and not necessarily in that order.

After a few more tries, the dozer finally coughed and sputtered its way into starting, and Mack continued deeper into the quiet woods.

* * *

Kevin stared up at the tall tree. He had spent ten minutes looking for a small one to start with, but none of the trees in this area was small by any stretch of the imagination. In fact, the smallest he could find was probably twice as tall as the tree he'd cut down earlier this week on National Forest land. Since no small tree was to be found, Kevin decided to take the opposite approach and searched out the tallest pine he could find.

Trying to run through every bit of advice Derek had given him, Kevin prepared to topple his second tree—his first legal one. Kevin fired up his saw and put it up to the tree in preparation to cut, then he remembered something he'd forgotten, and removed the saw from the trunk. He looked around until he found a suitable lane to drop the tree. Then he placed the saw against the trunk and started his first cut. At one point, Kevin's saw bogged down and he became worried that he would get hung up on the first cut he made on his first tree. He knew that the only why out of that bind was to have another sawhand, or flathead, come along and drop the tree for him so he could get his saw out. Not wanting to endure this shame, Kevin pulled back as hard as he could while keeping the chainsaw at full throttle. This course of action almost cost Kevin much more than a little embarrassment, as the blade came out of the tree suddenly and swung downward for his leg. Despite the fact that he released the trigger instantly and had all but arrested the whirling blade's momentum before it touched his leg, the saw still managed to cut through his leather chaps. He practically threw his saw to the ground and began frantically investigating his leg. Even his blue jeans under the chaps were torn, but miraculously his leg was untouched.

Kevin's stomach did a little turn as he ran his hand up his pants leg and wiggled his finger through the hole in both his blue jeans and his chaps. Now he understood the importance of the last bit of advice his friend had given him.

With newfound respect for his saw, he started again. This time he made both cuts without incident, then removed the wedge.

Kevin went around to the other side of the tree and started the last cut. The chainsaw blade buried into the tree, causing wood chips to fly. After he had sawed almost halfway through the tree he heard a series of popping sounds, and withdrew his saw.

As he watched the tree topple to the ground he was hit with an overwhelming urge to yell *timber!* at the top of his voice. He managed to keep from yelling, and thereby embarrassing the hell out of himself, but the very idea of making such an ancient proclamation made him laugh until he had to sit down.

After debranching and sizing down his first legal tree, Kevin went on to his second. After a few minutes this tree was tumbling to the ground, and he went to work preparing it.

Kevin was finishing up the uppermost branches of the tree when he noticed a small log cabin about a hundred yards ahead. Despite the distance, the lack of underbrush gave Kevin an unobstructed view all the way to the cabin, which rested in a slight incline that started where he was standing and continued to the other side of the cabin before rising back up into another smooth, wooded hill.

Curious, Kevin made his way over to the cabin.

He expected to find a dilapidated shack that had been long abandoned and was on the verge of collapsing in on itself, but this wasn't what he found at all. Once he got closer, Kevin realized that the cabin was in very good shape. There was no rotten wood, the ancient looking chimney still stood erect out of the roof without a single stone out of place, even the roof appeared to be in perfect shape.

The cabin looked peaceful. A shallow crystal clear steam trickled its way down the hill from Kevin's left and passed right before the house before disappearing between two hills to the right. There was a simple windowless door made of wooden boards with only a rope loop to serve as a doorknob. Two windows were symmetrically placed on either side of this door, with their shutters drawn open. The eaves of the roof stood out from the cabin sufficiently to cover the porch that ran completely around the house.

Kevin stepped over the trickling stream that was no more than a half a foot wide and maybe an inch deep at the most, then walked over to the house and stepped up onto the porch. When he did a cool pleasant breeze blew across his face that was a stark contrast to the hot and still summer morning he had been experiencing. The breeze felt good on his sweaty face, so he stood there for a while enjoying it with his eyes closed and a smile on his face.

Despite the presence of the gentle breeze blowing across his brow, no brush or branches moved with the wind. It was almost as if the breeze only existed on the porch. With his eyes closed and his face bent in a smile of idiotic bliss, he missed this entirely.

Kevin walked over to the door and pulled on the rope handle. The door opened smoothly, without the hinges making a single sound, and without the bottom of the door scraping along the floor, as is so common in old wooden houses. It was as if the house had been built to perfect precision and had stayed that way.

With the light coming in from the open windows, Kevin was able to make out the furnishings of the cabin. The inside was every bit as orderly as the outside. Its solitary room was immaculately clean, with very little furniture. There was a small wooden bed against the wall to Kevin's right, with a thin feather mattress, a thin feather pillow (both the mattress and the pillow were white and spotless, they almost looked like they had been bleached), but no sheets; a neatly folded quilt rested under the bed. Beside the quilt, about a half-dozen candles lay in a neat pile. A tall, thin, unstained wooden dresser stood in the far right hand corner, beside the bed. On top of this dresser were a mirror and a puddle of wax that had once been a candle. On this side of the bed there was a simple table that probably served as a nightstand; a solitary tin cup rested on the tiny table. On the far left side of the room there was a row of shelves that probably served as a pantry. Aside from another larger tin cup, a tin plate, a tin bowl, and a ladle, these shelves were bare. Below the shelves was a pair of cast iron pots, both of which were also exceedingly clean. The fireplace was in the left side of the room; inside, another cast iron pot hung on a bar that would have held it over the fire. There was a table in the center of the room with a lone chair pushed up to it. On this table was another candle that had been reduced to a puddle of wax, a jar of ink, a quill, and several sheets of paper stacked neatly before the chair. All of the furniture appeared to be handmade with the same absolute precision as the cabin itself.

Kevin looked down at the floor before he stepped in. The rough wooden floor was as clean as the rest of the house. It made him feel as if he should remove his work boots before entering. This he didn't do, but he did return outside, and stomp most of the excess mud off on the porch.

He returned to the door and stepped inside.

It felt cool inside. Not quite like air conditioning, and not cool enough to be alarming, just slightly cooler than it had been outside—in a word, comfortable. It was like the breeze on the porch, only without the wind.

He walked over to the table and looked at the paper. There was writing on the lineless paper. Without reading it, he picked up the first sheet and found that the writing continued through the next seven pages. He set the pages back down exactly as he had picked them up.

There was something about this place that made him think of it as some type of shrine, as if everything had to be in a certain place because that was just where it was supposed to be. It wasn't just the meticulous order and cleanliness of the place, but also the silence. It seemed like the reverent silence of a holy place, or maybe that of a tomb. Despite the fact that the one room cabin was quite small, it seemed that Kevin's footfalls had a slight echo to them. Perhaps it was the feeling of reverence toward the place, but Kevin felt that the sound of every footfall, the whisper of every breath, the rustle of his clothing, every sound he made, was a violation of some unwritten law. Mentally, Kevin pictured a twenty foot–tall cross between Paul Bunyan and Mrs. Thurman—the librarian back at his old high school—coming along and gently yet firmly picking him up to his/ her face and shushing him.

He walked softly over to the fireplace. There were no logs inside. There wasn't even any ash on the floor or soot in the chimney. It was clean, just like everything else.

While on that side of the room, Kevin took a look at the pantry. Upon closer inspection he found a tin spoon and a tin fork and a pair of large wooden spoons to go along with the cup, plate, bowl, and ladle he'd already noticed, but other than these items, the shelves were empty.

Kevin turned and walked out of the cabin, back out to the front porch, where he decided it would be nice to take a short break. He removed his work boots, then sat down on the edge of the porch, and enjoyed the cool breeze. A glance at his watch told him it was only 6:25; if he rested ten minutes he would have plenty of time to take down a few trees before the first break.

As he sat enjoying the breeze, a strange feeling slowly washed over him. Despite the pleasantness of his surroundings, there was still a twinge of an emotion that could only be labeled as fear coming on. It was like a feeling of being watched by something, not something far off and hidden in the woods but something not too far away.

Something very close.
Something right behind him.
Kevin spun around toward the cabin. Nothing.
A chill ran down his spine.

—Three—

WHAT THE HELL?" Don Elkins muttered as he passed by the place where he was absolutely positive the trail into the woods had been.

He geared the log truck down and began pulling over to the shoulder of the road. Behind him, a second log truck did the same.

"What's goin' on, Don?" a voice came over the C.B.

Don reached to the center console, grabbed the mike, and answered, "The road's here somewhere."

With the hiss of air brakes, the two log trucks came to a stop on the shoulder of the road. The first truck was the same one that had been by earlier to deliver the dozer and the skidder. Now this truck was carrying the crew's loader. Behind this truck was a second, equally dirty log truck that was carrying an empty log trailer, ready to be loaded.

"Big Mack, this is Don," Don said into the mike, "I'm having a little trouble finding the road. Send someone down in the pickup to lead me in. Over."

No answer, only static.

"Big Mack, this is Don, do you read me. Over?"

Still nothing but static.

"You sure this is the place?" Robert Morrow's voice crackled over the C.B.'s speaker.

"Positive," Don answered.

Don got out of the cab and walked a couple of steps toward the woods. There was no sign of the road that he had seen earlier marked with orange ribbons; in fact, there was no path or trail at all.

Robert had climbed out of his truck and was walking over to where Don was standing. "No road here, Don. It's either further up or we done missed it."

"No, it was right here," Don said, pointing at a spot in the woods where he *knew* the ribbons should be.

"I remember passing over the bridge, and it was just a couple more yards down. I know it was after Jimmy Haggard's place, and it was before John Miller's."

Robert walked on up to Don, gave him a friendly slap on the shoulder, and said, "Well, Don, I'm a lookin' and I just don't see no road. You sure you're on the right end of the county?"

"I was raised in this neck of the woods," Don said. "I'm tellin' you the road was right here."

"I doubt anyone moved it," Robert said with a laugh, and another friendly slap on Don's back.

Something had been bothering Don ever since he'd seen the road earlier this morning. The road had been only two miles from where he'd been raised, and he'd lived all his life within five miles of this place, yet he didn't remember a road being where this one had been this morning. Even if it had just been a path into the woods, Don was sure he would have remembered it, because he'd been hunting these woods ever since he was a boy, which was now quite some time ago.

Don turned to Robert, "Why don't you drive up a couple more miles and see if you can find the road, I'm gonna drive over to Aunt Jessie's and try to reach Mack on his cell phone."

* * *

While Uncle Butch was alive, Aunt Jessie never slept past five in the morning, but ever since his death ten years ago, she'd started sleeping on into the day, sometimes as late as eight o'clock.

Don knocked on the door for the fourth time, this time calling out, "Aunt Jessie, it's Don! I need to use your phone!"

No answer.

Don knocked again, and was about to call out for her when he heard a voice from inside yelling, "Hold your damn horses, I'm coming!"

Inside he could hear the slow clopping of her walker as she made her way to the door.

A couple more minutes passed, and the door opened revealing Aunt Jessie in all her glory. She was wearing a purple and red striped muumuu that was apparently designed by someone who had never been told that horizontal stripes are a no-no for obese people. Her face was in its usual wrinkled, toothless scowl. Around her neck was a neck-brace that she'd been wearing since a minor fender-bender three years ago. The brace had at one time caused the old woman's few unestranged relatives to give her a small amount of sympathy, so she had made it part of her everyday attire. She had failed to notice that the neck brace had ceased to work to her advantage roughly two days after she first put it on.

"What the hell is all the racket about?" Aunt Jessie said in the loud bellow that is so common among the hearing impaired, then she wheezed a couple of times as if the effort to say these few words had run her out of breathe.

"I need to borrow your phone."

"What for? You broke down or something?" Aunt Jesse said loudly, without giving any sign of moving out of Don's way.

"Or something," Don muttered, suddenly wishing he had stopped at his cousin John's instead.

"What?" Aunt Jessie bellowed.

"Mack didn't give us good directions to the site, so I need to give him a call."

"Now, how in the blazes are you gonna call Mack if he's out in the woods?"

"He's got a cell phone."

"Huh?"

"A cellular phone," Don said, raising his voice so she could hear him, "You know, a portable. . ."

"I know what a damn cell phone is!" Aunt Jessie snapped, and finally started going through the motions of moving her ponderous body from the doorway, "Just didn't know Mack was the type of man to have one of those damn machines."

Don started in the house but was arrested by Aunt Jessie's bellow. "Wipe your damn feet. I know your daddy taught you better than to come in a house without wiping your feet."

Don wiped his feet on the *Welcome* doormat, then continued through the door, past Aunt Jessie, and into the kitchen. He fished his wallet out of his back pocket and looked for the piece of paper he had written Mack's cell phone number on several months ago. After fumbling through dozens of scraps of paper and a few old lottery tickets, Don finally found the number.

He pickup up the phone and dialed. It rang a couple times, before a pleasant electronic voice came over the line and said, *"The person whom you are trying to reach is not available, please try again."*

—Four—

AT EIGHT O'CLOCK, Derek returned to the pickup for the first break. Roy and Mack were over by the skidder, taking a look at the engine, and Harry was sprawled across the pickup's tailgate looking awkwardly comfortable with his right leg propped up on the edge of the truckbed, his left arm and leg dangling from the tailgate, and his right arm lying across his brow to shield his eyes from the sun.

Kevin was nowhere to be seen.

"Where's Kevin?" Derek asked as he approached.

Harry, who was about half asleep, muttered something unintelligible and shifted his right leg a little before bringing it back to the same spot as before.

Derek stopped and listened. There was no buzz of a chainsaw, and it suddenly dawned on him that he hadn't heard one in Kevin's direction in quite some time.

He began to worry.

Logging wasn't exactly the safest job in the world—in fact, it could easily be labeled as one of the most dangerous. Many loggers been had hurt, crippled, or even killed due to a tree falling the wrong direction, or, worse yet, a chain coming off a saw to maim its operator. Derek had an ugly scar that ran up his forearm from one such accident.

"Harry!" Derek said, this time with much more emphasis.

"Huh?"

"Have you seen Kevin?"

"Naw," Harry drawled. He started to add something else, then he too realized how long it had been since he'd heard a saw in Kevin's direction. Harry sat up so quick it almost caused him to tumble off the truck's tailgate. He turned toward the skidder and called out, "Hey, Roy. You seen Kevin?"

Instantly Roy replied, "Aw hell."

He took off into the woods in the direction Kevin had gone, followed closely Derek and Harry.

Mack took his cigar from his mouth in a swift angry motion, then bellowed at Roy, "Damn it, Roy. I told you to keep an eye on that kid."

Mack jammed the cigar back in his mouth and took off after them.

Roy called out for Kevin a couple of times, and when he received no answer, he broke into a run. Pangs of guilt were welling up in the old skidder driver; he had been so wrapped up in the problems he was having with his skidder that he had forgotten all about checking on the green flathead. As he ran along he called out Kevin's name once more, but didn't stop to listen for an answer. After going only a hundred yards or so from the truck, Roy saw a massive fallen tree. There were no other trees down in the area, and Roy suddenly felt his heart sink. Either the kid had been killed, or he had been severely hurt on his first tree and had now been lying out here for the better part of two hours.

Roy stopped, cupped his hands to his mouth and yelled, no, screamed, "KEVIN!"

Instantly a not-so-distant, yet not-so-close, voice answered, "Yeah?"

Behind him, Roy heard Mack mutter, "I'm gonna kick his little ass. I swear on Momma's grave, I'm gonna kill the little bastard."

Roy and Mack had been working together for almost thirty years now. More than enough time for them both to develop standard reactions to each other's actions. The normal Roy-reaction to the Mack-action of declaring that he was *gonna kick somebody's ass* was to try to smooth Mack's ruffled feathers. Right now, however, Roy found that his nerves had been frayed to the point that the only thing that crossed his mind was, *not if I get to him first.*

"Where you at?" Derek called out.

"Down here!" Kevin called out, "Come look!"

The four of them set off in the direction of the voice, and soon they came to the rise that overlooked the cabin. Kevin was on his way up toward them. No one noticed the cabin—all eyes were on Kevin.

"You guys are never going to guess..."

"Were the hell have you been, and what the hell have you been doing, cause it sure ain't been cuttin' logs!" Mack bellowed as he started down the slope, "I hired you to do a job, damn it, and I expect you to do it!"

Kevin was speechless. Sure, he'd been loafing, and maybe Mack had a right to be upset, but he'd only taken a short break. Derek had warned him about Mack's mood swings. He had said that Mack had a bad temper, but this was ridiculous. It wasn't like he'd wasted *that* much time.

As Mack thundered down the hill, he took one last, powerful drag from his cigar, before tossing it aside like a bad habit. Mumbling obscenities as he came on, Mack walked up to Kevin and grabbed the boy by the upper arms. Pain shot through Kevin's biceps as the big man squeezed.

"What the hell do you think this is, a damn picnic?" Mack roared with his mouth barely an inch from Kevin's face. "What were you doing out here, because it sure as hell wasn't cutting logs?"

Kevin glanced over at Derek, hoping for help of some kind, but his friend suddenly found something interesting on the ground and avoided his gaze.

"Answer me, boy!"

"I . . . I saw that cabin . . . and thought I'd take a look." Kevin stammered in high-pitched voice that had been mothballed since puberty, "It hasn't been that long."

"Like hell! It's been two hours and you've only dropped one tree!"

This stunned Kevin—there was no way it had been two hours. He brought his left wrist up as high as he could and craned his neck until he could see his watch. It read, *6:36 a.m.*

"It's only six thirty." Kevin whined defensively.

"The hell it is." Mack said, and released his grip on Kevin's right arm so that he could bring his watch up into Kevin's face. It was far too close for Kevin to read, but Mack helped him out, "It's almost half past eight you stupid little shit."

Kevin's eyes finally focused enough to make out digital watch that was only inches from his face. Sure enough, it read *8:24 a.m.*

But there was no way that much time had passed. Surely he hadn't dozed off for almost two solid hours and not even realized it. And then what about his watch?

"My watch is wrong." Kevin said defensively.

Mack didn't even honor that comment with a reply. He released his grip on Kevin's other shoulder, as he did, giving Kevin a slight shove that sent him staggering backwards a couple of steps.

Mack turned to Derek, "Where in the hell did you find this boy?"

"He's an old friend of mine who was looking for work."

"Well, I can see why the little bastard wouldn't have a job. Probably can't keep one longer than a week." Mack growled, then he added, "You said he's experienced. Who'd he work for before me?"

"We've worked together on some small jobs on the weekends."

"Under who?" Mack pressed.

"It was just me and him." Derek said, carefully looking Mack straight in the eyes so as to give no hint that he was lying, "Small scale jobs, like clearing subdivision lots and cutting down dead trees in people's yards."

Mack snorted, "Well, he needs to go back to working those small jobs, 'cause I sure as hell don't need someone who cuts down one tree in two and a half hours."

Mack turned back to Kevin, "You'll finish up today 'cause I don't have the time to haul your ass back home, but I don't think we'll be needin' you come Monday."

With that Mack turned and started back up the slope followed by Roy and Harry. As he walked along he grumbled about the thirty-minute break they had just taken, and Harry mentioned that his watch said it was still only a couple minutes after eight. Harry immediately regretted having said this, as Mack lit into him with a verbal barrage that was only slightly less abrasive than the one that had targeted Kevin.

Kevin and Derek stood in silence for a couple of seconds, Derek watching the crew continue up the hill, Kevin watching his feet.

"It hasn't been two hours." Kevin finally said.

"It's been about an hour and a half at least." Derek replied.

Kevin raised his left arm and pointed at his watch's face, "It's only been a couple of minutes. Look." Kevin turned his arm so that Derek could see the watch.

Derek glanced at his own watch, "Sorry, bud. Your watch is off." Derek showed Kevin that his watch read straight up eight o'clock.

L   A   T   H   E   A   D   S

"His watch read eight thirty," Kevin said defensively.

Derek just shook his head.

"Well, he shouldn't've got so pissed off." Kevin said with a wild flair of his arms, "I'll make it up if I have to, but he didn't have to carry on like he did."

"You scared him, Kev," Derek replied with a shrug, "Hell, you scared me, too. You could've been hurt or even killed for all we knew."

Kevin tried to come up with a reply to this, but before he could Mack called out from up the slope, "Are you two going to get back to work or not?"

Derek and Kevin started back up the slope.

—Five—

THE CREW GATHERED BRIEFLY at the pickup before Mack sent the sawhands back out while he stayed behind with Roy to see if they could get the skidder running.

Kevin sullenly made his way back to where he'd dropped his only two trees of the day. He set his gas can on the stump of the first tree and looked around. Where was the second tree? The first one lay there in plain sight, all trimmed and ready to be loaded on a truck, but the one he had sawed next and had just started trimming before he noticed the house was nowhere to be found. Kevin walked the length of the first tree from the stump to the top. He remembered that the next tree was directly ahead of the first one. It couldn't have been more than a couple dozen feet from the top of the first tree to the stump of the next. But when Kevin got to the top of the fallen tree, there was no second tree to be found. He tried to convince himself he was just missing it somehow, but how do you miss over one hundred feet of fallen pine?

This troubled Kevin; in fact, he was becoming a bit scared. He looked around the pine forest and found it vaguely unsettling. Something just didn't seem right, but he couldn't put his finger on it. Kevin wasn't the woodsman that Derek was. Despite the fact that Kevin had lived in the area all his life, he had never been big on hunting, camping, or any other activities that involved the millions of trees that surrounded his hometown. On mornings that his buddy Derek had been sitting in a box stand waiting on that trophy sixteen-point to step out from the brush, Kevin had been curled all snug in bed and generally wouldn't rise until well after the time that Derek would have come out of the woods, sometimes with, but usually without, a deer. On weekends that Derek and some of his other friends had bought a couple of cases of beer and lugged a couple of tents into the woods, Kevin had never failed to show and even stay the night drinking and talking. But the next morning Kevin's hangover would drive him home before he'd spent the first sober hour among the pines. Perhaps if Kevin had spent more time in the woods he would have missed the call of the mockingbirds, the chatter of the squirrels, or noticed that no mosquitoes buzzed hungrily around his face. Perhaps he would have noticed the fact that the wind was completely calm—dead calm—yet the pinestraw that littered the ground rustled constantly and occasionally took flight into the air. Perhaps he would have noticed how the shadows were much darker and longer than they should have been, or how the sun still had failed to show itself despite the fact there wasn't a cloud in the sky and sunrise had been quite some time ago—depending on whose watch you went by.

Then again, perhaps these details would have evaded Kevin even if he had made all those early morning hunting expeditions and stayed on into the next day when his friends camped out. Around two hundred yards to his left, Derek was having similar bad feelings about the woods, but, despite his experience, he was unable to pin down what it was that bothered him. Over a couple hundred yards to Kevin's right, Harry was too concerned about running out of snuff to notice anything peculiar about the woods. And directly behind Kevin, Mack and Roy had all their attention directed toward finding out what was wrong with the skidder.

Kevin didn't stand around for long; he didn't want Mack to come back and find him twiddling his thumbs.

Kevin set his saw on the ground, and gave the cord a pull. The little engine chugged once, but didn't fire. The next time he pulled the cord, it didn't even do that. Kevin tried three more hard pulls before turning the choke on, and trying again. He gave five more hard pulls, but still the engine refused to fire. Kevin turned the choke off; the last thing he wanted to do was to flood the engine.

He frantically tugged in vain a dozen or more times before grabbing his hardhat and tossing it to the ground with a loud, "Damn it!"

The last thing Kevin wanted to do was have to go back and have someone start his saw for him.

Then he noticed a sound in the distance. He could hear a series of brief grinding noises coming from Derek's direction. It was the sound of Derek trying to crank his saw. Apparently he was having similar problems. Kevin turned in the other direction and listened, and, sure enough, he could hear the same sounds coming from

Harry's direction.

Kevin smiled. Mack couldn't get mad about him not being able to start his saw if everybody else was having the same problem.

Then Kevin's smile faded—why wouldn't their saws crank?

"Okay, that's it." Kevin muttered to himself, "I'm quitting. I don't care if I have to walk home, I'm getting the hell out of these woods right now."

Kevin picked up his hardhat and put it back on his head, then he grabbed his saw and started back to the truck with the sound of Harry and Derek's uncooperative saws grinding away in the distance. Before he made it back, both of these sounds had stopped as Harry and Derek either gave up or noticed that no other saws were running and started back to see what was going on.

Mack saw Kevin making his way back to the truck. "And just what do you think you're doing?"

Kevin walked slowly as he made his way back to the pickup while he thought of how he was going to go about quitting without getting squashed by *Big Mack*. But as he walked along, Kevin decided that it was time to suck it up and be a man. He decided that he would boldly tell Mack that he quit, put the saw and all his gear in the back of the truck, then walk back down the road to the highway where he would thumb a ride home. This is what he planned, anyway. But when Mack asked what he was doing, he didn't tell him he was quitting - boldly or otherwise. The only thing he managed to say was, "Uh . . . my saw won't start."

Mack started lumbering toward him, "Son, if you broke my saw, I'm gonna take it out of your ass."

"Mine won't start either, Mack," Derek said, as he stepped around the truck. He nodded in the direction that Harry was supposed to be cutting and added, "And from the sound of it, Harry's not having much luck himself."

Mack stopped and glared at Derek. "Bullshit."

Then he continued over to Kevin, jerked the saw out of his hand, and commenced pulling on the cord. It didn't fire. Mack lifted the saw to his face and smelled, "Gas." he said, as he glared at Kevin, "Probably flooded."

"Try mine," Derek said, and Mack started his way.

Mack pulled away at the cord, but the saw's engine wouldn't so much as turn over once.

Just as Mack set Derek's saw down, Harry stepped into view and said, "Aw, don't tell me ya'll're havin' problems too."

Mack tossed his cigar to the ground, "This is bullshit . . . bullshit! There's no way all three of these saws ain't workin'."

"Not to mention the skidder." Roy added.

"And where's Don?" Derek added. "He should have been here an hour ago."

Mack was about to reply with another bout of vulgarity, but he was interrupted by a long peal of thunder. The weather in East Texas is known for being unpredictable, but this was downright strange. Mack and Roy both kept careful tabs on the weather, and they knew that it was supposed to be dry as the Sahara for at least a week. Not only that, but there wasn't a cloud in the sky. Or was there?

One by one, starting with Mack, they turned their heads to the sky. Menacing black clouds hung just above the treetops.

But those clouds hadn't been there earlier.

Large raindrops started tumbling their way to the ground, slowly at first, but the rain began steadily increasing.

"Rain," Roy muttered the obvious. "Everybody in the truck."

Harry and Derek put their saws and equipment in the back of the pickup. Seeing this, Kevin followed their example. After covering the equipment with a tarp, they all climbed in the cab of the truck. They all got situated in their seats then turned in silence toward Mack, who was still out in the weather. Oblivious to the rain, he stood looking up at the sky. After a couple of minutes, he started to the pickup.

"I doubt this is gonna blow over," Mack said as he climbed behind the driver's seat, "Guess we'll call it a day."

All eyes were on Mack's big right hand as he put the key in the ignition. He turned the key and the engine fired without missing a lick.

"At least somethin' around here works." Mack muttered as he put the truck in reverse.

Mack turned the wheel all the way to the right and backed the pickup between a pair of trees. Then he shifted to drive, turned the wheel in the other direction, toward the road he had widened just a couple of hours ago. But when he straightened the pickup out, there was no road to be seen. Only the sound of the hard rain on the roof of the pickup broke the silence as all five men scanned the woods with their eyes, searching for the missing road.

"It's rainin' too hard." Mack said, "I can't find the road. Anyone else see it?"

No one answered, only the steady drumming of the rain on the roof.

"Someone needs to get out and see if they can find the road."

Without a word, Roy opened the door and walked to the front of the pickup. From there, he looked around, but couldn't see any sign of the road. Everybody watched in silence as he walked further out, and continued on, become harder and harder to see through the rain, until he couldn't be seen at all.

Five terribly long minutes passed.

A brilliant show of lightning forked its way across the sky and was followed almost instantly by a roll of thunder that built to such a crescendo that the truck was vibrating before it was over.

Another minute passed, and another show of lighting lit up the sky.

Everyone was intently looking ahead, trying to see Roy through the veil of rain.

"There he is," Harry said from the back seat. He leaned over the front seat and extended his arm, pointing almost directly ahead. "By that tree."

In the front seat, Kevin thought he saw Roy as well. He just could see a vague human outline among the trees. Only this outline seemed much taller than Roy, and it wasn't searching for a path in the woods, it was standing in one place. It appeared to be facing the truck, watching them.

"Where?" Mack asked. "I don't see him."

"Aw, shit. He's gone now. He was right over..."

Suddenly there was a loud pounding on the window of the pickup's left rear door. Everyone, including Mack, jumped and turned toward the door.

"Goddamn it, open up."

It was Roy. The left rear door on Mack's pickup was bad about locking itself from time to time, and apparently when Roy had left it had done just that. Harry quickly opened the door, and Roy climbed in, soaking wet.

"Well?" Mack asked, after giving Roy a little time to get situated.

"Can't find it."

"What do you mean you can't find it?" Mack growled.

Roy shook his head and replied, "I can't find it, Mack."

"Damn it," Mack swore and flung his door open and stepped out.

As before, everyone watched as Mack disappeared into the rain. A couple of minutes later, Mack returned and climbed into his seat without saying a word. No one asked if he had found the road. They already knew the answer and didn't want to further agitate the already grumpy bear.

Mack reached down and turned on his C.B.. There was slight click as he turned the knob, but no static came forth.

"Damn!" Mack swore.

Then he reached across to the glove box, giving Kevin, who was sitting in the middle of the front seat, a minor jostling with his elbow as he did. In the glove box, Mack found a small cellular phone, and took it out. The cell phone was one of the newer models and wasn't much bigger than a pager. Even when it was folded open, the phone was almost swallowed by Mack's massive hands. Unlike the C.B., the cell phone came on, but that was all it did. Across its small screen the phone read, *NO SIGNAL*. Mack tried to dial a number anyway, but only got static.

"This is too weird." Kevin said with a slight tremble in his voice, "I mean, first all the chainsaws and the skidder stops working. Then a storm blows in from nowhere, we can't find the road out and the C.B. and the cell phone quit working."

"Oh quit sounding like such a damn titty-baby," Mack said. "I've seen storms blow up like this before, and as far as the machinery, we probably just got a hold of some bad gas. And we're probably walking right past the road and not seeing it—hell, it's rainin' like a cow pissin' on a flat rock out there. The C.B.'s as old as the hills, so it was due to break down at any time, and this piece of shit," Mack said, holding the cell phone up so everyone could see it, "never works out in the woods." With that, Mack squeezed the cell phone, until its plastic shell cracked and popped under the pressure, then he threw the shattered phone into the floorboard. "We'll just wait the storm out." Mack continued, "There's no reason to go and start being a baby."

Mack had no sooner said this than the truck died.

—Six—

IT WAS MISERABLE INSIDE the cab of the truck. When the truck had died, it failed to recrank, leaving the five men without an air conditioner, and, with the temperature hovering just below one hundred degrees, it was like an oven, or rather a steam cooker since the sudden downpour had drastically increased the humidity. Not only was the sticky heat a problem, but, contrary to the commercials that showed a half-dozen or so linebacker-sized men climbing in and out of a four door dually similar to Mack's, the conditions in the pickup were quite cramped, especially for Kevin. Wedged between Mack and Derek in the front seat, Kevin had no room at all to stretch out his legs. The only way he could think of to get comfortable was to put his feet in one side of the floorboard and lean up against the person on the other side of the truck. The problem with this was that he would have to decide whether he wanted to play footsy with or snuggle with Big Mack, who was still quite obviously in a terrible mood. Kevin decided that he would just have to stay uncomfortable.

Then, almost as if the powers that be were trying to prove to Kevin that things could get worse, the top of Mack's windshield began leaking all along the right side of the truck, slowly soaking Kevin and Derek's legs with steady drips of water. Not long after Kevin and Derek gave up on shifting their legs around in an effort to find a spot that the water wouldn't drip on them, Harry started snoring. It was just a light growl accompanied by an occasional snort at first, but soon it sounded like Harry had managed to get one of the chainsaws working and was trying it out in the back seat.

For two hours the rain continued to pour down. Soon Roy dozed off, and added his wheeze-like snoring to Harry's chainsaw. With even less room to move around, no one in the front was able to sleep. Mack started becoming more and more agitated.

If Mack Barton were to ever find himself on a shrink's couch, there was little doubt that he would be diagnosed with a serious case of bipolar disorder. When he was in a good mood, the big man could be as jolly as they came, but when his moods turned sour—and they were prone to change in a moment's notice—the man became downright mean.

Mack reached under his seat and brought out a half-empty pint of vodka. After removing the top he brought the bottle to his lips and took a long pull, then he put the top back on and placed the bottle on the dash. The bottle sat there for less than a minute before Mack grabbed it and took another drink.

Mack then started getting restless and fidgety. Every now and then would grunt a few cuss words under his breath as he shifted his weight trying to find a more comfortable position.

One particular shift of his position caused his knee to connect with the steering wheel. "Damn!" Mack bellowed.

Roy jerked awake immediately, and Harry snorted a couple times, smacked his lips, then went back to sawing logs.

"Aw, screw this," Mack said. He took a cigar and a lighter from his shirt pocket and lit the cigar without as much as cracking the window. He turned toward the passenger's side, looked Kevin dead in the eyes, and said, "If you don't like it, you're more than welcome to sit in the no smoking section." He hiked his thumb over his shoulder. "It's back there in the bed of the truck."

With that Mack blew a puff of smoke into Kevin's face.

Kevin didn't say a word in reply. It was all he could do to keep from coughing. He knew if he did, it would probably only encourage more abuse from Mack. Kevin turned to the front and watched out of the corner of his eye, as the logging boss chugged and puffed on his cigar as if he was in some great hurry to fill the cab of the truck with as dense of a layer of smog as possible. The cigar smoke in the cab got thicker and thicker, but no one dared say a word, not even Roy.

Kevin began to think about the cabin back in the woods. Since it didn't seem like the rain would let up any time soon, he began to think it might not be such a bad idea to seek shelter there. It would be quite a long run through the rain to get to the cabin, but considering how much more room, and less cigar smoke, the cabin offered, it would probably be worth it. The problem was, Kevin was afraid to say anything for fear of Mack jumping down his throat.

L   A   T   H   E   A   D   S

After taking a good five minutes to build up his nerves, Kevin turned to Derek and said, "I saw a cabin back where I was cutting. It's probably a lot dryer than here. Why don't we go wait out the storm there."

Derek opened his mouth to answer, but before he did, Mack spoke. "If you found some cabin off in these woods, it's probably as old as the hills and got a lot more leaks than this truck."

"Actually, it looked pretty new," Kevin replied. "It's probably someone's deer camp."

Mack returned to puffing his cigar.

"That sounds like a winner," Derek said. "Do you mind, Mr. Barton?"

"Hell, no," Mack replied. "It'll give me more room to stretch out. You two be sure and listen for a horn though. When Don shows, I'll get him to blow for you."

Derek nodded, then turned to the back seat. Harry's head was leaned back on the seat with his mouth wide open. He was snoring away. Roy, on the other hand was slumped down with his head in his hands. Mack's outburst had woke him, and the cigar smoke was preventing him from returning to sleep.

"You want to come, Roy?" Derek asked.

Roy looked up at Derek, then glanced to the roof of the truck where a thick layer of smoke was slowly swirling. His eyes were already red and puffy from the smoke. There was little doubt that he'd much rather be anywhere but in the pickup; however, he replied, "Naw, I'll just stick around here."

"Okay, I offered," Derek said, then he turned to Kevin. "About how far are we gonna have to run through all this rain?"

"It wasn't very far from where I dropped my second tree," Kevin replied.

If anyone else noticed that Kevin mentioned cutting down a second tree, they didn't say anything. But just bringing the tree up made Kevin wonder, once again, just what happened to that tree. This rekindled other questions about just what exactly was going on out in these woods. Why wasn't the equipment running? Why couldn't they find the road?

Kevin had begun to have serious second thoughts about running through these strange woods, but his friend made his mind up for him.

Derek grabbed the door handle and flung the door open. He stepped out of the pickup and turned to Kevin. "You lead the way."

Kevin paused; he wasn't so sure about this.

"Come on, damn it," Derek said, "I'm getting soaked."

Kevin slid out of the pickup and set off in the direction he had been cutting earlier. Kevin ran along at a fast jog, with Derek with behind him. It wasn't long and they came to the first tree Kevin had cut down—of course, the second one was nowhere to be found. Once Kevin started down the depression that was just past this fallen pine, he thought he could make out the cabin through the pouring rain, but he wasn't sure. Then, while Kevin's eyes were searching more for any sign of the cabin than they were looking for good footing, Kevin slipped on a muddy patch of ground. His feet went right out from under him and he went sprawling on his chest. Derek, who was too close behind him to slow down, attempted to jump over his fallen buddy. He was successful in the jump, but his landing quickly turned into a stumbling lope that carried him four more long strides down the hill, before he too went down on his chest.

Kevin spit three times to clear his mouth of mud and pinestraw, then he called out "You okay?" as he regained his feet.

A few more feet down the hill, Derek rolled over into a sitting position, and started laughing, "Whose idea was this anyway?"

Kevin joined in the laughter as he made his way over to help his friend to his feet. As he pulled Derek up, he saw the cabin just ahead.

"There it is!" Kevin shouted, and he started that way at a much more cautious pace.

Soon they were standing on the cabin's porch, alternating between laughing and panting as they tried to catch their breath.

They had almost quit laughing when Derek suddenly started again. Between guffaws, he was able to spit out, "You should've seen yourself. It was like one minute you're running, the next you're eating dirt."

Kevin resumed his laughter as well, "You weren't exactly swans in motion yourself." Then Kevin went through an exaggerated imitation of Derek's pinwheeling arms as he tumbled down the hill.

They continued joking and laughing back and forth for a few more minutes before Derek turned and looked over the outside of the cabin, "Not bad."

"Yeah, it's a nice place to visit, but I wouldn't want to live here."

Kevin reverently stomped his muddy boots off, and Derek did likewise, then they proceeded inside the cabin. Kevin walked through the door first, followed by Derek. The only light was provided by the open windows, so, with the dark storm clouds overhead, it was considerably darker inside than it had been during Kevin's earlier visit.

"Well, it's certainly no deer camp." Derek commented as he stepped over the threshold and into the one room cabin. "There's no beer cans scattered all over the place."

"Surely no one lives here," Kevin said.

Derek didn't answer at first, he just looked around the cabin. After a couple of minutes he replied, "It sure is well kept. And if this is a deer camp, it's different than any camp I've ever seen. Those things usually sleep about a dozen or so men, and drunk hunters certainly aren't this neat." Derek turned toward the table, grinned and said, "There wasn't three bowls of porridge on that table when you came in was there? Cause if three big-ass bears show up and start spouting off about 'who's been eating my chow' or shit like that, I'm haulin' ass outta here."

Kevin laughed. "No, but there was old woman with a wart on her nose who told me she was looking for a pair of German brats named Hansel and Gretel."

"This must be where she cooks the kids," Derek said walking across the floor to the fireplace. As he did, he drew his arms tight to his chest. "Damn, it's cold in here."

Kevin had also pulled his arms tight, "Yeah, there's like a draft in here or something. I doubt being soaked to our underwear helps either."

Derek checked out the fireplace then walked back over to the table. "What's this?"

"It's some sort of note." Kevin said as he checked out the bed, thinking seriously about stretching out in it for a good long nap.

"It's older than it looks. I didn't get a chance to read it, but it's dated nineteen-seventy at the top of the first page."

"Uh, Kev, old buddy," Derek said, picking up the first page and examining it closely, "This doesn't say nineteen-seventy; it says eighteen-seventy."

"Oh, bullshit," Kevin replied as he sat down on the bed. "There's no way that paper would be in that good of shape if it was over century old. It'd be all yellow and crinkled. Hell, it'd probably have fallen apart when you picked it up."

"Maybe so, Mr. Historian, but did they write with a feather and a jar of ink in the nineteen-seventies?"

At that, Kevin got up and walked over to have a look at the paper that Derek held in his hands. Sure enough, it read July 15, 1870, in the upper right hand corner.

Derek handed the paper to Kevin, and said, "Read it. It'll help pass the time. We sure ain't got anything better to do."

"If you want it read, why don't you read it?" Kevin said with a smirk. "Unless you've managed to go illiterate since high school."

"Naw, I jes' wanna hear a purdy-mouth college boy read it to me," Derek said, grossly exaggerating his Texas accent. "Po country foke like m'sef don't get to hear many a college boy talk. We don' see many a those in these here parts."

While Kevin laughed, Derek walked over and sat on the bed. Kevin plopped down in the single chair in front of the table and looked over the paper. There was just enough light for him to make out the words on the page, but not enough for him to read by without great difficulty.

"Reach under the bed and grab one of those candles," Kevin said.

"What candles?"

"They're right beside the quilt."

Derek reached under the bed and felt around. "I don't...here they are." Derek brought a candle out from under the bed, looked it over, then tossed it to Kevin. With the cabin as dark as it was, Kevin didn't even try to catch the candle. He quickly put his hand over his face, and the candle hit him softly in the shoulder then fell to the ground.

"Nice catch," Derek commented as Kevin scooped the candle

from the floor.

"Screw you." Kevin said. "Now *hand* me your lighter."

Derek reached in his pocket, took the lighter out, and tossed it to Kevin. "Heads up."

Again Kevin defensively put his hand over his face, and the lighter lightly struck him before falling to the ground.

"Have you ever thought about playing outfield for the Astros?" Derek commented.

"Have you ever thought about jumping off a cliff?"

Kevin flicked the lighter repeatedly, but it wouldn't light.

"You're not going to believe this," Kevin said, as he continued flicking the lighter, sending tiny sparks flying that briefly caused warped and twisted shadows to appear on the cabin's walls.

"Is it empty?"

Kevin paused his flicking and shook the lighter. He could hear fluid inside. "Nope."

"Maybe it got wet."

"Maybe," Kevin commented as he held the lighter close to the candle's wick, hoping that one of the sparks would be sufficient to do the trick. Finally, just as Kevin was about to give up, a spark managed to land in the right place and a tiny red ember appeared on the end of the wick. Kevin blew lightly on this glowing speck until it increased to a tiny finger of flame.

"Success!" Kevin commented. Then he looked around and noticed how eerie the room looked in the candlelight. The shadows seemed to ebb and flow with the candle's flicker, almost as if they were breathing in unison.

"Kinda spooky, ain't it?" Derek said as he stretched out on the bed.

"Yeah." Kevin answered dreamily, as he watched the breathing shadows on the wall. Considering all the weird things that had happened today, he figured he had a right to be a little on the skittish side.

Kevin watched the shadows for a few more seconds, then he turned back to the papers and started reading.

—Seven—

July 15, 1870

It is with a trembling hand that I write my tale.

I was employed by a Dr. Samuel Rutherford of Boston Massachusetts to assist in surveying a large tract of land that he has recently purchased in Texas. Rutherford purchased this land through his agent, a Mr. Rufus Lowery, a resident of Galveston who claimed familiarity with all of the land in the eastern portion of Texas. That he knew his trade, there is little doubt. However, this villainous Southerner had no interests save his own in mind. He informed Dr. Rutherford of the vast woodlands to the west of the Sabine River, and convinced the doctor that this area had yet to be logged only because of the backwardness of the people residing in the area, but now that the area was being reformed under the helpful hand of the Government of the United States the area would soon become one of the most important sources of timber in the country. This was an outright lie. The area is completely without any river deep enough to float logs, nor is there any industry in the immediate area that could use the timber; furthermore, the forest in the area is almost entirely made up of worthless Southern Pine; a gummy wood as worthless as the people residing in this God forsaken land. Mr. Lowery arranged the sale of ten-thousand acres of such land to Dr. Rutherford at a criminally high price. Dr. Rutherford, having no reason to distrust his own agent, thought that the price was fair considering all he had been told, and went through with the purchase of the land. As soon as the deal was done, and the money had exchanged hands, Mr. Lowery disappeared, no doubt with his pockets well lined with Dr. Rutherford's hard earned money, as well as a sizable sum from the former owner of the land in question.

Having swore he would never do business directly with a Southerner again, Dr. Rutherford contacted myself to represent his interests abroad. During the war, I had served with the doctor in the Thirty-second Massachusetts before his transfer to the medical staff of the Army of the Potomac, and I had maintained correspondence through the remainder of the war and the years following. At the time I received Dr. Rutherford's letter, I was becoming quite bored with my job as an editor of the Boston

L   A   T   H   E   A   D   S

Trumpet. Therefore, I jumped at the opportunity to represent the doctor in his affairs. Two days after receiving the letter I met with Doctor Rutherford to work out the exact nature of my assignment in Texas. The doctor informed me that he had invested quite a bit of money in this worthless land, far too much to simply accept the loss. He needed someone to survey the land and see if there was any way that the land could be divided up and sold at a profit. He was aware that on average, the local populace was quite poor, and the few wealthy residents of the area had lost most of their fortunes during the war, making it all but impossible to sell the land to the natives of the area. However, the doctor designed to convince the district commander to purchase the land for the resettlement of freed Negroes. If that plan fell through, the doctor instructed me to trade the tracts of land for confiscated cotton, hoping their sale in foreign ports could help lessen his financial loss.

After receiving my directions, I booked passage from New York to Galveston on the steamer Hattie Smith. On the fifth day of June, less than one week after first meeting with the doctor, I arrived in Galveston Harbor. Upon my arrival, I immediately started preparations to survey the land that Doctor Rutherford had been swindled into purchasing. Justifiably wary of trusting native Southerners, Dr. Rutherford had instructed me to hire a Northerner who was familiar with the area to serve as my liaison. For this purpose, I hired a Lieutenant John Flint, who was currently on leave from the Federal garrison at Galveston. Lieutenant Flint proved perfect for the task; not only was he exactly the type of man the doctor had instructed me to hire, but he was also a skilled cartographer, enabling me to fill two much-needed positions with one man.

Lieutenant Flint and I then proceeded north to Jasper, the closest town of any size to the doctor's land. There, Lieutenant Flint introduced me to a Mr. James Moore, who knew the area in which we were to be traveling. Mr. Moore struck me as an ignorant buffoon, but Lieutenant Flint swore to me that not only did he know the area like the back of his hand, he had fought on our side during the war and was completely worthy of our trust. Before setting out, we also hired the services of two Negroes, Jerrod and Eli. They proved to be hard workers, but their years of forced servitude had weakened their will to the point that they had developed an annoying habit of fawning and pleading at the slightest hint of displeasure, especially if Mr. Moore raised his voice or his hand. The very sight of the interaction between these three sickened me, as it seemed to serve as a perfect shadow of the foul institution of slavery.

From Jasper, we set out north-by-northeast on a wagon trail that wound through the forest in the direction of Milam, another tiny eastern Texas town. We traveled some fifteen miles on this trail before we entered the area that Dr. Rutherford now owned. For eight days we remained in the area, mapping out the doctor's land.

On the morning of the ninth day, Eli began to show signs of illness. He was sweating profusely, running a high fever, and complaining of stomach cramps. I offered to cut the expedition short and return to Jasper to allow him medical attention, but Eli refused, claiming it would pass. However, by noon the next day, Eli's symptoms had increased to the point that he was having fainting spells, and was quite delirious when conscious. We attempted to make our way back to the trail, but Mr. Moore's compass had begun spinning wildly, and Mr. Moore soon informed us that we were lost. At first I believed that Mr. Moore had lost our way out of spite for the poor sick Negro whom he didn't have the least bit of respect. In fact, I had a heated argument Mr. Moore to that effect that came to my drawn pistol and his drawn knife, and probably would have left one of us or both of us dead had it not been for Lieutenant Flint, who stepped in and separated us. Toward the end of the day, our troubles took a turn for the worse, as a storm suddenly and unexpectedly blew in.

It was while seeking shelter from the storm that we found this cabin. At first we thought it to be a wonderful stroke of luck, but now I feel that it was the work of the Devil himself that brought us here.

During the night, Eli's fever rose until he began having what we assumed was hallucinations. He screamed like a banshee throughout the night, saying that the demon of the woods was coming for us. I tried my best to calm the poor Negro, but his rantings became worse as the night grew longer. At roughly midnight, he became so wild that he had to be forcibly restrained to prevent him from hurting himself. At first we tried to restrain him by holding his arms and legs to the bed, but his strength was many-fold due to his insanity. The only way we were able to keep him to the bed was by cruelly binding his hands and feet behind his back, yet, even in this condition, he managed to throw himself from the bed onto the floor.

While Lieutenant Flint, Mr. Moore, and myself were struggling frantically with Eli, Jerrod was going from window to window in the

L   A   T   H   E   A   D   S

cabin, watching and listening. When we finally secured Eli, Mr. Moore demanded an explanation from Jerrod as to why he had been of no help during our struggle with Eli. Jerrod explained that he had heard something moving around outside and feared that it was the demon that Eli was seeing in his feverish waking nightmares. Mr. Moore commenced to giving Jerrod a tongue lashing, and I am ashamed to say that Lieutenant Flint and I sided with Mr. Moore. I had always been told that coloreds were a superstitious lot, so I assumed that Jerrod was either imagining hearing this demon, or perhaps he was making up the tale so he wouldn't have to handle a person that was behaving as one possessed by the Devil. Under Mr. Moore's constant verbal abuse, Jerrod begged forgiveness for not helping with Eli, but he continued to insist that he had heard something outside the cabin. I professed not to believe a word that either of the negroes had said, yet, after the argument died down and we all turned in for the night, I found myself straining my ears throughout the night, trying to decipher between the sound of the rain falling and other sounds that made their way to my ears.

By the next day Eli's condition had worsened until he was completely comatose. We were afraid to move him for fear that the exertion would be too much for his weakened constitution. Jasper was less than a day's walk, so we decided that Mr. Moore and Jerrod would go back and return with a doctor the next day. Since I had a minimum amount of medical training, I was to stay behind with Eli, and Lieutenant Flint was to stay behind and assist me. Mr. Moore and Jerrod set out not long after daybreak. Throughout the remainder of the day, Eli remained comatose. I watched him closely for any sign of improvement, but none came. I feared he was at death's door. Nevertheless, Eli lasted through the day and on into the night.

It was around ten o'clock that Eli's condition took a brief and strange turn. No longer fearing that he was going to get up and hurt himself, we had freed him from his restraints and laid him comfortably on his back. Since nightfall, Eli hadn't so much as moved a muscle, not even a reflexive twitch, then, suddenly, while the lieutenant and I were in conversation at the table in the center of the room, Eli's entire body tensed, his eyes flew open and, in a voice that was flat, unaccented, and certainly not his own, he spoke the words, "It draws near." The very moment these words had left Eli's lips, the poor Negro was dead.

It was but moments after Eli's dark declaration and subsequent death that a piercing scream cut through the forest. Lieutenant Flint swore this scream sounded like Mr. Moore, but I argued that this was impossible, since he should have been far away from the cabin by that time. Even if we had been somewhat lost at the time we found the cabin, Mr. Moore had assured us that he would have no trouble finding the road by using the direction of the morning sun to travel eastward. Lieutenant Flint agreed that Mr. Moore was too experienced of a woodsman to have wandered around in a circle and made it no further than within shouting distance, but he insisted that the scream had sounded just like Mr. Moore.

That night, both the lieutenant and I became aware of the sound of movement outside. My first reaction was that Mr. Moore and Jerrod had returned, but, having been made uneasy by the scream earlier in the night, I kept my pistol in hand and stayed inside.

Early the next morning Lieutenant Flint and myself buried Eli, then discussed our next course of action. Lieutenant Flint suggested that we wait at least one day for Mr. Moore's return. I had become somewhat uneasy about the cabin, but I saw the merit in the lieutenant's idea. Neither of us were very knowledgeable about the surrounding area, and, since it had already been proven that even one so knowledgeable as Mr. Moore could lose his way, it would make sense for us not to attempt to set out on our own. The rest of the day was spent playing cards, and trying to divert our attention from the strangeness of the last couple of nights. This task proved simpler than we imagined, as time seemed to pass quite hastily that day.

That night the sounds of movement became undeniable. At one point we even heard heavy footsteps walking along the porch. We tried to catch a glimpse of our unwelcome guest as it passed the windows, but it always seemed to pass just outside of our sight at the very moment we turned our eyes, leaving us with only the vague impression of something quite large. After the footsteps made two complete circles around the cabin, they paused at the door. The Lieutenant Flint and I readied our pistols, and I called out that we were armed. Slowly the door creaked open to the width of approximately one inch. Not knowing whether we faced beast or man, I tipped the table over for use as shelter against possible gunfire. The door slowly creaked open another inch or so, then stopped. We waited for a sudden rush on the door, but it never came. The footfalls never picked back up, making us believe that whatever or whoever was outside our door had remained there, so we stayed behind the table with our pistols pointing toward the door for the better part of the night. It was almost morning before Lieutenant Flint and I built up the courage to advance on the door. He stood ready, while I stealthily walked over and grabbed the door-handle. I flung the door open, not knowing exactly what to expect, but certainly expecting some form of a life or death struggle. What greeted us at the door was only the slow, cold wind. Our antagonist had departed.

The next morning we decided to cut our wait for Mr. Moore short. We set out shortly after sunrise, planning to walk east, into the sun, as Mr. Moore had. We continued for what seemed to be only thirty minutes or so, but when I looked up at the sun, it was almost directly overhead. I checked my timepiece, and found that it read a quarter past eight. I brought this to the attention of Lieutenant Flint, and he agreed with me that it seemed the watch was right, but it was certainly impossible that the sun could be wrong. We walked at a brisk pace, but it seemed that every time we looked up the sun was much further toward the western horizon than it should have been. Lieutenant Flint then suggested that we go back to the cabin, he said that we'd be much safer there from whatever it was that we had heard the night before. At first I wanted to press on, but one glance at the setting sun, told me that the lieutenant was right.

The sun continued its rapid descent as we briskly made our way back to the cabin. Soon I began to have the distinct feeling that we were being watched. I never said as much to Lieutenant Flint, but I could tell by the way he suddenly picked up his pace that he was under the same impression. We continued after the sun had set and began to hear movement all around. It was never continuous nor was it ever in the same spot twice. By the time twilight gave way to dark, we were thoroughly unnerved by this constant stalking from every direction and began running through the woods like frightened children. We had made no effort to mark our passage, so I was fearful that in the dark we would miss the cabin altogether. However, we practically stumbled onto the porch without having to search around for landmarks. Once again, I thought us lucky, but now I know this not to be the case.

Once we were in the house, we began frantically preparing ourselves for an attack from whatever it was that had harassed us the night before and stalked us in the woods that very night. The table was once again tipped over for use as cover, and all the shutters were closed. At first, our visitor didn't make its appearance, then we began to hear movement outside. This continued for some time before whatever it was stepped up on the porch. It walked slowly toward the door and, as with the night before, stopped there. We watched anxiously while the door creaked open about an inch and stopped, just as the night before. At this point, the tension got to Lieutenant Flint. He'd had all he could take, and was determined to end this standoff once and for all. He sprang from around the table, rushed to the door, and flung it open. As he did, he pulled the trigger, but his gun failed to discharge. The lieutenant saw whatever it was at the door, and screamed. I could see nothing but a hulking outline. As I rushed forward to lend my assistance, something reached out and struck Lieutenant Flint, propelling him across the room. Though I did not get a good look at the creature in the doorway, with the lieutenant out of the way, I took aim at its outline and attempted to dispatch the vile beast back to hell with my pistol, but, as with the lieutenant's firearm, my pistol failed to discharge. I slammed the door, and leaned my body against it, trying to prevent the vile beast from entering our sanctuary. I cried out for Lieutenant Flint to give me assistance, but he just sat leaning against the far wall staring down at the place where the creature had struck him. There was a smoking hole that had burned through his clothes and singed the skin underneath. The Lieutenant lay looking at this strange yet minor wound with wide staring eyes. I continued calling for his assistance, but still he sat, staring and not saying a word nor moving a muscle to lend me any assistance.

Realizing I was on my own I braced for the creature's assault, and soon it came. It began with a slow yet strong push on the door. With my back to the wall and my feet braced as best I could, I leaned back into the door, preventing the creature from entering. This went on for some time, during which I noticed that my back was growing warm, as if a roaring fire was heating the door from the other side. The next morning I would find severe burns and blisters all along my back and shoulders, but in my frantic state at the time I knew only warmth, not realizing pain. Then the pressure on the door ceased for the span of a couple of minutes. No sooner had relaxed my guard than something slammed forcefully into the door. Fearing that I couldn't hold against this new, much stronger assault, I began screaming at Lieutenant Flint for assistance, but he only gazed at me from across the room, as if I were a total stranger speaking in a foreign tongue. I held the door against three more brutal assaults, each stronger than the next. I knew that the next assault would break me, but still I stood with my back to the door, awaiting the blow. Lieutenant Flint finally joined me at this point; without uttering a word, he set his shoulder to the door just as the next blow was landed. Two more blows came, each stronger than the next, then there was silence. The rest of the night passed quietly.

The next morning, yesterday morning as it was, I could not get Lieutenant Flint to tell me what he had seen at the door. At my every inquiry, he just shook his head and answered with silence. We then discussed another attempt at walking out, but decided that yesterday's expedition had proved that such an attempt would be futile. We then made what little preparations could be made against the assault that we knew would be coming that night. We tried our pistols and found that each and every bullet we had misfired. The only weapon at our disposal was the lieutenant's knife, and a makeshift spear that was made by sharpening the end of a long stick. As night grew closer, we moved the bed over by the door, then tipped it up for use as a brace. We then got what little sleep our shattered nerves would allow. We awoke well before dark, then, with the bed propped against the door, my makeshift spear in my hand, and Lieutenant Flint's knife in his, we waited for the night, which wasn't long in coming.

That night the beast came almost as soon as darkness fell. The struggle was horrific. Time and time again, it slammed into the door, each time with increasing ferocity. We held our ground at first, but eventually one of the blows caused the bed to fall to the floor. By then the blows were landing on the door with such rapidity that there was no time for us to reposition the bed, and without the bed's assistance, each impact caused the door to widen a little further. Soon Lieutenant Flint, who was closest to the opening of the door, cried out that it had him. I looked over and could see that his right arm had been dragged through the door, and something was attempting to pull him outside. The assault on the door ceased, as the creature turned its attention to dragging the lieutenant out of the protective confines of the cabin. I likewise ceased leaning against the door, grabbed Lieutenant Flint's other arm and tried to pull him back inside. The lieutenant screamed repeatedly that his arm was on fire, and pleaded with me to pull harder, but I was pulling as hard as I possibly could, and still Lieutenant Flint was being drawn slowly through the doorway. He was fully halfway out the door, when the creature gave a heavy tug that caused me to lose my grip on poor Lieutenant Flint's arm, and he was suddenly propelled out the door. I shudder as I recall the screams I heard just outside the cabin. These screams continued for quite some time while I lay on the floor weeping. No more attacks came on the door that night. Whatever was out there was satisfied with one victim, for the time being, anyway.

At some point during the night, I fell asleep from sheer exhaustion. I awoke to find myself alone in the cabin. Outside there was no trace whatever of Lieutenant Flint. Resigning myself to my inevitable demise, I have seated myself at this table and taken up pen to write out my tale. Come nightfall I shall step outside and meet my fate.

Brian L. Kinney

—Eight—

THAT'S TOO WEIRD," Derek commented from the bed as Kevin finished the story.

"Yeah, you could say that," Kevin said, taking a long look around the dark candle-lit room.

Seeing the look of concern on Kevin's face, Derek said, "It sounds like a load of bullshit to me. Someone's probably playing a prank on us or something."

"Pretty elaborate prank. I mean, every piece of machinery we've got stops working, and trees that we've cut down get right back up."

Derek's head jerked up at this, but he said nothing.

"What?" Kevin asked.

"Nothing." Derek replied, laying his head back down.

"No, you were going to say something weren't you? Did you have some trees that you thought you had cut down wind up standing the next time you looked at them?"

At first Derek said nothing, then he murmured, "I thought so, but I probably just miscounted."

"Well, I cut down two trees," Kevin said holding up two fingers, "How many did you see when ya'll came and checked on me?"

"You probably just forgot where it was."

"Bullshit, I cut this one down right next to the first one, but when ya'll showed back up there was only one tree. Don't tell me I miscounted either, because I'm pretty damn sure I know the difference between one and two."

Derek didn't say a word. He could see what Kevin was talking about. Everything that had happened today had been really out of the ordinary, and this note really put the icing on the cake. There were even quite a few similarities between the story that Kevin had read and what was happening to them, the rain, for one thing, and the fact that they just happened to stumble on this cabin out in the middle of nowhere. Another thing that bothered Derek was the fact that he'd seen no signs of life since they arrived: no birds, no squirrels, no deer tracks, nothing. But Derek kept this to himself, if he told Kevin this, it would add fuel to the fire. Derek felt that he needed to keep his cool, and he knew if Kevin started freaking out, there was a good chance he would join right in.

"So you did have trees get back up on you?" Kevin asked.

"No, Kevin, I miscounted, and you probably threw the tree in a different direction and lost track of where it was."

Kevin started to interrupt, but Derek held his hand up.

"In the woods, it's easy to lose your direction," Derek continued. "You usually can't see the sun until it's straight overhead and pine trees tend to look alike. All it would've taken was for you to think the stump was a couple yards in the wrong direction, then drop the tree away from where you're looking, and you've managed to lose an entire tree. As far as the equipment goes, we might have gotten a hold of some bad gas. Mack buys all his gas from Peterson's and if he's got a bad leak in his gas tanks it would've affected the truck, the skidder, the dozer, and even the saws."

"The skidder and the dozer run on diesel."

"If something caused water to start leaking into Peterson's underground gas tank, then it might have caused water to leak into the diesel tank as well."

"What about the C.B. and the cell phone?"

"Like Mack said, the cell phone was a piece of shit, and the C.B. was old as the hills."

Kevin thought about this for a minute, then came back with, "Okay, then explain how the road went missing, and why the storm blew in all the sudden."

Derek laughed. "Come on, Kev. You've lived here all your life. You know how unpredictable the weather is, and we couldn't find the road because it was raining too hard. Hell, Mack probably got lazy when he was dozing the road, and didn't make it wide enough to find even without the rain."

"Well, how do you explain this letter," Kevin said, holding the pages of the note up and shaking them.

Derek thought for a moment, then said, "I'm not sure, but you said yourself that there was no way it could be a letter from the eighteen-hundreds, 'cause it looks too new. I think that proves right there that it's a fake and we can't believe a word in it."

L   A   T   H   E   A   D   S

Kevin sat the papers back on the desk and looked them over once again. It was all too much of a coincidence, but the alternative was simply unthinkable.

Hearing himself explain the situation helped Derek considerably. He rolled over so that he was facing the wall and said, "If you don't mind, I'm gonna try and make the best of cheating you out of the bed and get a little nap."

Kevin didn't answer

It wasn't long before Derek's breath evened out and he was asleep.

Kevin found it impossible to make himself comfortable in the hard straight-back chair, so he stood up and walked to one of the windows to watch the rain. It was cloudy out, so it was hard to tell, but Kevin could swear that it seemed much later than it really was.

—Nine—

THERE WASN'T A CLOUD in the sky when Don drove the log truck past Mack's shop and on up the driveway to the house. With a loud hiss of airbrakes, he pulled up behind Mack's wife's car.

Don didn't get out immediately, though. He slumped forward on the steering wheel, and massaged his temples as he chewed lightly on the inside of his bottom lip. This was the classic Don-in-deep-thought pose, normally reserved for the morning crossword puzzle (when he had time for it, anyway), but today his problem was much more serious than finding a four letter Scandinavian city than ends with an O. Don had spent the better part of the morning searching for the road that he knew the crew had gone down earlier that morning. At noon, after hours of driving up and down the roads looking for the orange flagging, he had returned to Mack's shop. When the log trucks failed to show up at the site, Mack would come back out of the woods to find out why. Don knew that this meant an ass-chewing when the boss returned, but it seemed like it was the only way he was going to find the site. But Mack didn't show back up at the shop. After waiting a couple more hours, Don set out again, this time to check out all the bars and hangouts within a thirty-mile radius. Of course at three in the afternoon, none of these places would normally be open, but, since Mack was on a first name basis with the majority of the owners, Don thought it might be possible that he had talked someone into opening up early. Still, Mack was nowhere to be found. By the time Don finished checking out all the honky-tonks, the sun had gone down. After one last pass by where he could have swore the road had been, Don headed back to town. He had fully expected to see Mack's work truck parked in its customary place beside the shop, but, once again, it was nowhere to be found.

Don sat in the cab of his truck thinking his way through the details of the day, trying to figure out how he could have misplaced a logging crew, and why Mack hadn't come looking for him. He probably would have sat there, chewing on his lip, for an hour had it not been for the front porch light coming on, ripping him away from his thoughts.

Don opened the door to the truck, and slid down to the ground.

In spite of the fact that Mack made a pretty good living, his house was simple in the extreme. It was a wooden two-bedroom house that was propped off the ground by eight semi-evenly spaced stacks of bricks. The house appeared to have been painted white at one time, but was currently in dire need of another coat or three.

The yard was in a similar state of disarray. There were no shrubs or flowerbeds; instead, there were several rusted out log truck bodies and one ancient skidder that hadn't run in twenty years. In the spring, the Bartons' yard turned into a soupy quagmire; any step off the cracked concrete walk could cause a person to lose a shoe in the ankle-deep mud. Right now, however, the yard was as dry as a bone; it had been one of the driest summers Don could remember, and it certainly didn't look like there would be any rain in the near future.

As Don made his way up the walk, the front porch to the Barton's house opened, revealing Mack's wife, Loretta Barton. The tiny curly haired woman stood in the door with one hand on her hip and the other propped on the doorsill. Her eyes were squinted into narrow slits, and her lips were pursed around her cigarette as she inhaled deeply. She had a look about her that said she'd rather take a baseball bat and beat the hell out of a person than say hi. It was a common joke around town that the reason Mack and Loretta Barton had gotten hitched was because she was the only woman who could be just as mean as him. Don knew that this wasn't really the case. Mack had a bad temper, especially when he was hitting the bottle, and he could sometimes be a bit of a bully. But Mack did have his good moods, and there was a limit to his temper. His bark was generally worse than his bite. He might bellow and cuss at a person, but he seldom used his fists unless pushed to do so. Loretta, on the other hand, had a vicious bite that often showed up without the least bit of a warning. The little woman was just plain old mean.

"Have you seen Mack?" Don asked as he approached.

"No, should I have?" Loretta answered sharply, her cigarette bobbing up and down in her mouth as she spoke.

"We had a little trouble today, and the trucks never made it to the site," Don explained, "I figured he'd have come looking for me when I didn't show, but he didn't."

Loretta took another drag from her cigarette as she gazed down at Don from her elevated position in the doorway as if he were some sort of bug. "The bastard's probably off drunk somewhere," she finally said, "It wouldn't be the first time he's screwed up a day's work 'cause he wanted to go off drinkin' and whorin'.."

"But all his hands' cars are still here." Don said, motioning over his shoulder toward the shop where Don's employee's vehicles were all parked. "Surely he would have dropped them off if he'd...uh... gone out."

"Shit, Don, he probably took them with him. Roy and Harry are alcoholics just like he is, and that kid's a damn thug—he probably had Mack drop him off so he could buy some dope."

Don had the information he needed, so he simply said, "Thanks." and started back to his truck without waiting for a reply.

* * *

Don was greeted at the door by a yapping toy poodle whose actual name was Mary Belle, but who he had always called Stupid. At one time Don had hated his wife's little dog and the dog seemed to have similar feelings toward him. However, when Annette had died in a car accident four years ago, Don had found himself becoming attached to the little poodle, and Mary Belle in turn seemed to have a change of heart about him. It seemed that they both were reaching out to each other, the last remainder of their beloved Annette.

"Hey there, Stupid!" Don said to the poodle as she bounced up and down, still barking away, "How's my little bitch?"

Don kneeled down, and Mary Belle/Stupid immediately ran across the living room to get her favorite toy - a tiny white teddy bear. Once she had the bear, she turned and started back to Don so fast that her little legs skittered on the slick hardwood floor at about twice the speed she was actually moving. She scampered over and jumped into his arms.

"How's Stupid, Jr. today?" Don asked as he grabbed the bear and tugged lightly, causing the poodle to growl playfully and rapidly shake her head. He continued playing for only a couple more seconds before setting her back down. "I've got some calls to make," he explained.

Don got up and started across the living room toward the kitchen. Not pleased with the small amount of attention she'd received, Mary Belle/Stupid continued barking—in a muffled tone due to the fact that Stupid Jr. was still in her mouth—and jumping up and down alongside Don as he walked toward the kitchen.

In the kitchen, Don took the wall-phone and dialed Roy's number from memory.

"Hello?" Sue, Roy's wife, answered after the first ring.

"Sue, this is Don. Roy wouldn't happen to be there would he?"

"No, he hasn't come in yet. I was just about to call you and see if you'd seen him. I'm beginning to get worried. It's not like Roy to stay out this late without calling."

There was a moment of silence as Don debated telling Sue what had happened today. But he knew that Sue was one of the world's greatest worrywarts, and if he told her that the crew had gone missing, she'd have him riding the roads looking for them again.

Noticing the pause, Sue asked, "There's nothing the matter is there?"

"No," Don answered, then made up something off the top of his head as quickly as possible, "I left before he did and didn't get a chance to ask him if he could give me a hand changing the transmission on that old jeep I bought."

"Oh," Sue said, then she started with the questions. "Did y'all have to work far out of town today?"

"Not all that far, just about three miles south of Fairmount."

"Did you talk to them on the C.B. before you left? I mean, Mack would have told you if something had happened to Roy, wouldn't he?"

"Yeah, he'd've let me know first thing."

"Were they very far off the road?"

"It was a little ways back, maybe a mile."

"Mack wasn't drinking was he?"

"I don't believe so."

"Do you think they were having trouble with the skidder again?"

"No, he just finished rebuilding the motor, and it's been working like a charm." Then Don realized that this might be his chance to end the question barrage, so he changed his tune, "But now that you mention it, he did say it had been hard to crank this morning. I'll bet the skidder broke down and him and Mack are working on it at the shop."

"Oh," Sue said, then she turned this over in her head, her ever worrisome mind come up with an angle that this could be turned into a crisis. "Should I call over at there and see if he's okay?"

"They're probably outside and can't hear the shop phone and if you call the house, Loretta probably won't get up off the couch to check and see if they're down there, much less go down to the shop to tell Roy he's got a phone call."

"That's true," Sue replied.

"I hate to cut it short, but Stupid's telling me she needs to go out."

"Okay, but promise me you'll call if you hear anything from him."

"I promise. Gotta go, bye."

"Good-bye."

Don clicked the receiver, but didn't put the phone back in its cradle. He ran his finger down a list of numbers tacked to the wall beside the phone until he came to Harry's number. He dialed it. After letting it ring nine times, Don clicked the receiver again. He thought briefly about calling Derek or Kevin's parents, but decided against this idea. Sue was bad enough. He didn't want to tell a couple of parents that their kids, who had only been out of the nest for less than a half-dozen years, were missing. The last thing Don wanted was for Mack to show back up and find that Don had not only failed to find the work site, but had also roused the parents of two of his employees into calling the law to search for him.

Don hung the phone back up, and walked down the hall to get ready for bed. Mack had to show back up eventually.

Once he had settled in and Mary Belle/Stupid had snuggled up between his feet, Don closed his eyes and attempted to sleep, but sleep was nowhere to be found.

In fact, he was wide-awake when Sue called him around midnight and asked him if he'd heard from Roy. This time Don couldn't bring himself to lie to Sue. He told her what had happened, and by twelve-thirty, he was on his way over at her house to pick her up so they could go looking for the site.

—Ten—

NOT LONG AFTER NIGHTFALL, Kevin took the quilt out from under the bed, stretched it out on the floor and lay down on it. The sound of rain on a roof had always made him sleep like a rock, but not tonight. Laying on his back, listening to the sound of every gust of wind, his subconscious mind trying to bend that sound into some monster stalking around the cabin, while his conscious mind refuting this and declaring it was just the wind. When he finally began crossing the bridge between consciousness and sleep, he seemed to linger forever on that threshold. Warped images of reality that were twisted through his dream-kaleidoscope continued to surface as he attempted to drift, somewhat reluctantly, into sleep. At one point, he distinctly heard his mother calling him in for supper. Her voice had a haunting quality to it that made his eyes water beneath their closed lids. It wasn't the voice of his mother calling him in while he was in on summer break from college; it was the sound of her calling him in from the backyard swingset; it was the sound of her voice as it had been almost two decades ago. Not long after his mother's voice faded away, his mind ceased its loitering on the consciousness bridge and crossed on over into sleep.

At some point in the middle of the night, Kevin awoke to a sound just outside the door. Thunder? The wind? Something else? He didn't know he'd heard, but he knew he had heard something, a slight rustle just off the edge of the porch that didn't exactly fit with the steady droning of the rain on the roof. He listened closely, but heard nothing but the rain—it was still pouring outside.

Kevin felt around for the candle that he had snuffed out before he went to bed. Finding it, he then searched the pockets of his blue jeans—which he had taken off and rolled into a pillow—for Derek's lighter. Once again, the lighter wouldn't work, so Kevin began flicking it over and over, trying to light the candle on one of the sparks. One of the sparks almost caught, but the tiny ember went out before it could be nursed to a flame.

This ember had just died when Kevin distinctly heard three

footfalls on the porch. They seemed to walk from a place just on the other side of the door to the edge of the porch and then presumably onto the wet ground surrounding the cabin, where further steps would be muffled by the pinestraw and hidden in the sound of the falling rain.

Kevin clambered to his hands and knees and scurried through the darkness to the corner of the room, where he assumed Derek still lay sleeping in the bed. Not realizing how small the cabin really was, and thinking the bed was further away, Kevin ran headlong into the corner post. He winced and grabbed his head, and managed to keep from letting out any expletives.

"Kevin?" Derek said groggily.

"Shh," Kevin shushed quietly. "There's something out there."

"Oh, please," Derek said. Nevertheless, he too spoke in a whisper.

"Listen."

Derek did. They sat there for some time listening to the rain, but that was all.

"Okay," Derek whispered, "If this is some lame attempt to get the bed, then you're…"

Then the rain suddenly lightened, and he heard something. It was faint, but he could hear the muffled sound of footsteps seemingly coming from just off the porch. They seemed to walk along the edge of the porch, then stop at the corner of the cabin.

"You heard it!" Kevin whispered excitedly. "You heard it, didn't you?"

Derek didn't say anything. He was still listening.

The footfalls weren't long in coming. They started where they left off, then became fainter and fainter as they withdrew from the cabin.

After waiting for a couple more seconds to see if they would come again, Kevin whispered, "You heard them. I know you did, damn it, so don't deny it. There was something out there."

"It was probably the guys trying to scare us," Derek said in a voice that was scarcely louder than the whisper he had been talking in earlier.

"Oh, yeah, sure," Kevin whispered sarcastically, "They walk

around the cabin in the pouring rain for a while then leave without a good old-fashioned 'boo'. That really sounds like those crazy nuts you work with."

"It worked didn't it?" Derek shot back. "You're scared shitless."

"Screw you."

They sat there in silence for a little while longer, then Kevin whispered, "Scoot over."

"The hell I am!" Derek replied in as close to a normal voice as either of them had gotten so far.

"You've had the bed to yourself all through the day and for most of the night, and I've been stuck on the damn floor," Kevin whispered as he climbed onto the edge of the bed and started pushing Derek to one side. "It's not like we haven't shared a bed before."

"Yeah, but this is one hell of a small bed," Derek complained; nevertheless, he scooted over and made room.

After they got settled down, the two boys lay in silence for quite some time before either was able to drift off to sleep. Derek lay on his side with his eyes wide open for some time even after Kevin dozed off. There was no way what they had heard outside was one of the others, and he knew it.

* * *

Not far away, in the cab of Mack's pickup, all three men were sound asleep. Harry's chainsaw snore had been joined by Mack's deep baritone not long after the big man had snuffed out what remained of his cigar and stretched across the front seat. After a couple of minutes, Roy's nasal snore was added to the fray, making it a trio.

Roy had been asleep for quite some time with his head tilted back so that he was facing the ceiling, with his mouth wide open. Without waking entirely, he closed his mouth, and smacked his lips before tilting his head toward the door and resuming his snoring. Caught in an awkward position, it wasn't long before his neck muscles began cramping in protest. Roy's eyes blinked rapidly as he woke up and straightened his neck. He stretched his mouth wide in a yawn and looked at his watch. It read just a quarter past five, but he knew that was impossible, because it was pitch black outside. Roy slumped further down in the seat, and, since they would be here for the night at least, he tried to get back to sleep. Roy turned to his left, toward the window again, but this time he turned his whole body rather that just his head so that he could sleep without getting a cramp in his neck.

As Roy closed his eyes, he caught a glimpse of something just outside the window. The glass was foggy and streaked with rain, but he could still make out the outline of large head on the other side of the window so close to the glass that its breath had melted a pair of semi clear spots in the foggy window in front of its nostrils. Roy could tell that whatever was on the opposite side of the window was built like a human, but bigger. It seemed to be stooped down so that its face was inches from the glass, which was, in turn, only inches from Roy's face. Roy's eyes widened, and he opened his mouth to scream, but his voice seemed to be caught in his throat. Frantically he pushed himself away from the window and on top of Harry.

Finally he found his voice, "Oh-my-God, oh-my-God, something's out there!"

Harry awoke in mid snore, and immediately went into a choking fit, and Mack sat straight up in his seat and roared the first word that came to mind. "Damn!"

Roy continued frantically pawing his way away from the window on his side of the truck, even after he saw whatever was on the other side of the window rise up and walk away.

"What in God's name has gotten into you?" Mack yelled.

"S-something was outside the window," Roy stammered, as he finally quit his panicked flailing, and settled down into Harry's lap. "I swear to God, there was something out there looking in at me. It looked kinda like a bear or a big man and it was looking right through the window. Right at me."

"Have you finally lost your marbles?" Mack said. "Jesus Christ, you think you see something out in the rain and you start acting like a baby cryin' for his momma."

Underneath Roy, Harry had finally slowed his choking enough to say, "You're crushin' me to death here. Get up."

Roy got up and moved back to his side of the seat, the whole time looking at the window where he'd seen that massive form looking in at him. "I'm tellin' you I saw something big lookin' right in the window at me."

"You saw your damn ugly reflection. There ain't nothin' out there."

Roy said nothing. His body was still rigid, and he was still staring wide-eyed at the window.

Mack noticed the haunted expression still on Roy's face. "Good Lord," Mack said in a disgusted voice as he opened the driver's door and stepped out into the rain. Standing in the open doorway, he looked around the truck, then he leaned back in and said, "See nothing's out here."

Roy fully expected something to suddenly jump Mack from behind while he had his back turned, but nothing did.

Mack climbed back in the pickup, and shut the door.

—Eleven—

THE HEAVY RAIN CONTINUED beating down on the roof of the pickup throughout the night. It let up briefly not long before sunrise, but then was replaced by a brief yet furious hailstorm. Mack swore furiously as he saw the dents developing on the hood of his truck, but he also knew that, considering the size of some of the ice balls that were bouncing and rolling off the hood, they were lucky the windshield was holding. The hail quit falling after only about five minutes, but the rainfall picked back up as soon as it stopped. Just after sunrise another attempt was made to find the road, but with the visibility still cut to a couple feet by the pouring rain, they were once again unable to locate it. The rain then continued hard and without interruption until around noon, when it lightened up considerably but still didn't quit entirely. By then the three men had been sitting in the pickup for over twenty-four hours, although their watches swore that it had been more like twelve to sixteen hours, depending on whose watch was checked.

"Let's get out and try to find that damn road again before the rain picks back up," Mack said.

All three men got out and began systematically combing the area, looking for any sign of the road. They looked for a good thirty minutes before giving up and returning to the truck, drenched to their underwear.

"Looks like we're here till it quits," Roy, who was the last one to give up, said as he climbed in the pickup and shut the door.

"Like hell." Mack swore, "You may be enjoying this shit, but I'm fresh out of vodka and cigars, and neither of you two bastards have a decent set of boobs."

"If we can't find the road, how are we going to get out of here?" Roy asked.

"We'll walk out. We know the road's not far to the east, we'll just head out in that direction."

"I don't know, Mack. You know how easy it is to get turned around in the woods. Maybe we should just wait it out. Someone's bound to come for us when the rain lets up."

"Now you know I never get turned around," Harry drawled. "East's that'a way."

Harry did have an uncanny knack for knowing which direction was which; in fact, Roy had never known him to be wrong. But it wasn't just getting lost in the woods that Roy was worried about. He didn't say as much because he knew the ridicule that he would receive from Mack, but Roy was convinced that something strange was going on. As if the odd happenings of yesterday combined with whatever it was Roy had seen (he'd just about convinced himself it was a bear) weren't enough, last night they had found that all of their watches had begun to work erratically; it seemed that the hands on the watches were moving much slower, perhaps as little as two-thirds their normal speed.

"What about the boys?" Roy asked, reaching. Trying to come up with anything that would keep him from having to make a long walk through these woods.

Mack pushed down on the center of the steering wheel, but the pickup's horn was apparently broke like everything else.

"We oughta leave their sorry asses." Mack said, then he added, "I guess one of us could try to locate them and let them know we're walking out."

There was a brief silence then Mack and Roy turned to Harry, who had lost interest in the conversation and begun watching the droplets of water as they formed on his window. Noticing the silence he turned back and saw that his coworkers were staring at him. "Huh?"

"You're the damn pathfinder," Mack said. "You go."

"Go where?"

"Find the boys, shit-for-brains. Did your brain take a vacation?"

"Uh, naw," Harry said. "Where are the boy's supposed to be?"

"At some cabin that Kevin boy found while he was goofin' off," Mack said.

"He said it wasn't far from where he dropped his tree," Roy added.

Harry thought for a little while, then said, "Maybe if we left them a note."

L   A   T   H   E   A   D   S

"No, Harry, damn it," Mack said. "We can't just go and leave 'em in the woods."

"Well, I don't know if I can find the cabin. I mean it's not like I've ever been there."

"Jesus Christ," Mack muttered as he shook his head and turned back forward to let his head rest on the steering wheel.

"I'll go with him," Roy offered.

Mack didn't raise his head from the wheel to reply. "Okay, y'all scat." He gave a dismissive wave of his big hand.

Roy and Harry got out of the separate sides of the truck and walked around to the tailgate. The rain had lightened even more and was now just a steady drizzle, giving the air a hot murky texture. They started off in the direction the boys had disappeared the night before.

They made it no more than a few feet before they heard the pickup door shut behind them.

"Hold on," Mack said.

Roy turned and saw Mack making his way around the truck.

"I might as well stretch my legs a bit," Mack said.

They all headed off in search of the cabin.

* * *

Derek sat in the chair with his chin resting in his hands. A yawn escaped his mouth, but he wasn't really tired, just bored. Due to the fact that both Kevin and Derek's watches had quit working, it was impossible to tell how long Derek had been sleeping, but it had definitely been at least twelve hours. Now he sat in the cabin's chair wishing he could go back to sleep for lack of anything better to do. He had never been big on rainy days—sleep was about all they were good for in his book—but at least when he was stuck at home on a rainy day he could watch TV. This cabin had no modern comforts at all. Out of boredom, he had taken one of the pages of the strange note, flipped it over, and doodled all over the back of it, using the quill and ink. This page was now absolutely covered with his name—which was written several different times, in several different styles—and a poor rendering of a tattered Confederate battle flag. Derek had never been much of an artist. At the bottom of the page a message was written in huge slanting letters: *I'M BORED!* The page had now lost its interest and sat all but forgotten in front of Derek. He had considered waking Kevin to give him someone to talk to, but Kevin was sleeping pretty sound and he didn't want to disturb him. Not only that, Derek knew that if he woke Kevin up, the conversation would eventually turn to the strange predicament that they were in, and Derek was trying to think about that as little as possible.

Derek looked down at the much-scribbled piece of paper and had an idea. He picked up the paper and made a couple of folds until he had made a long, narrow paper airplane. When he was finished, he set the airplane on the table and looked it over. He chuckled as he realized the fact that this was probably the first time he'd made a paper airplane in ten years.

After he finished the preflight inspection, Derek picked up the plane, drew back and launched it in the direction of the Iraqi headquarters—that is, the bed—in hopes of taking out Saddam Hussein, a.k.a. Kevin Harvey. Since the bed was only around ten feet away, it was hard to miss. The point of the plane hit Kevin on the cheek, causing him to sleepily swat at his face without waking.

Finding this amusing, Derek immediately began the construction of *Derek Monroe Stealth Bomber II.*

Derek hadn't even made the first fold when he heard voices coming from somewhere outside. A momentary impulse of fear caused his pulse to quicken; for a brief moment he imagined that whatever they thought they had heard last night was coming for them. Then he realized that it had to be one of the crew coming to tell them that they'd found the way out.

"Hey, Kevin," Derek said as he stood. "Someone's here."

Kevin had been sleeping like a rock, and didn't respond in the slightest to his friend's voice.

"Kevin, wake up."

Kevin stirred somewhat, but didn't wake up entirely. He rolled to face the wall.

Derek walked over to the bed, grabbed Kevin by the shoulders and gave his friend a hard shake. "Wake up, Kev. Someone's here."

"Huh?" Kevin slurred as he raised his head from the pillow.

"Someone's here," Derek repeated. "They probably found the way out and they're comin' to get us."

Outside, Derek heard footsteps on the front porch. A couple of hard knocks came at the door, then, without waiting for an answer, the door opened and Mack stepped inside, followed by Roy and Harry.

"You two fags through playing house and ready to get the hell out of here?" Mack said with a grin.

Mack's mood had made one of its trademark about-faces during the walk through the woods toward the cabin. He had even been whistling as he walked down the slope to the little cabin.

Kevin swung his feet out of the bed, and tried to shake off the sleep-fog in his mind.

"Off and on," Mack said, in his shorted version of the oft-used phrase, *off your ass and on your feet.*

Derek and Kevin exchanged glances.

Mack noticed the exchange and the troubled expressions on their faces and said, "Don't tell me you two are going to start that shit about getting lost in the woods. I've already been through that with Roy. Harry never gets turned around in the woods, and the road is to the east of here. Probably only a mile or so. I'm sure it's less than three."

"I don't know if trying to walk to the road is such a good idea," Kevin said after a brief pause to build up his courage.

"Oh, for Christ's sake, why not?" Mack said in an exasperated tone.

Kevin walked over to the table and proceeded to tell Mack all about the letter they had found. He carefully pointed out the similarities between the situation described in the letter and their current situation. Then he gave them a recap of all the strangeness that had taken place over the last couple of days.

When Kevin finished, a strange expression came over Mack's face. It was a look of sincerity that didn't quite fit what Kevin had seen of Mack's personality so far.

Mack walked over to the table, picked up the papers, and looked them over.

"One's over there." Derek said, pointing at the paper airplane lying beside the bed.

Mack ignored him. He glanced over the first page of the letter but didn't read it. He set the papers back on the table.

"I'll admit there's been some weird shit happen the last two days, and maybe, just maybe, there is something a little out of the ordinary going on here," Mack said in a steady tone that matched his sincere look, "But I'll be damned if I'm gonna just sit here and wait for someone to come get me."

"Those people died," Kevin said, pointing at the letter on the table, "Something killed them. We even heard something walking around on the porch last night."

"It doesn't matter," Mack said, shaking his head. "I'm walkin' out. I don't for one moment believe that there's some sort of East Texas Bigfoot out there waitin' to eat me, but if there is I'd still rather try to get out than just stay here and wait for him come get me."

Mack looked over at Derek. "I suppose you're stayin' too."

"Yeah."

"Suit yourself," Mack said, surprising both boys with the fact he wasn't angry. "I'll come back tonight and get y'all and the equipment. It'll be easier to find the trail from the Highway." Then Mack turned to Harry and Roy. "Y'all ready?"

While Kevin and Mack had been having their discussion about the current situation, Harry had been absently picking at a blister on his thumb. Roy, on the other hand, had been listening with extreme interest. While Kevin had given his shortened version of the story that was in the letter, Roy's eyes had grown larger and his expression more troubled as the story continued. When Kevin mentioned that they had heard something walking around the cabin last night, Roy's mouth had dropped open.

"I don't know, Mack," Roy said. "Maybe we should wait. They heard something creeping around, and . . . well . . . I saw something last night too. If there's something out there, we'd sure be a lot safer if we stayed here."

Mack's sincere look faded from his face. "Are you gonna start that shit again? There wasn't anything out there."

"I'm tellin' you, I saw something," Roy pleaded. "And they heard something moving around."

"We're in the woods. It could've been a deer or somethin'."

"What I saw wasn't no deer."

L   A   T   H   E   A   D   S

Mack threw his hands in the air, "Fine. Stay here." Then he turned to Harry, "Come on, unless you've decided you want to stay too."

Mack turned and walked out the door, followed by the other four men. Mack and Harry stepped off the porch and into the drizzling rain. They continued on their way toward the slope, but Roy, Derek, and Kevin remained behind, watching from the porch. Mack and Harry made it to just the other side of the stream before Roy sighed heavily, then stepped off the porch after them. At a half-walk half-jog pace, Roy quickly caught up with the other two men. When he did, Mack turned to him, grinned and said something that caused Harry to burst out laughing, then Roy replied something that made Mack tilt his head back and laugh heartily.

Back on the porch, the sounds of this exchange were lost in the mist.

Kevin and Derek stood wordlessly at the edge of the porch as they watched the three men make their way up the rise, then disappear over the crest.

—Twelve—

THE RAIN STOPPED ENTIRELY not long after the three men left the cabin and set off into the woods with Harry in the lead. However, the droplets of water falling from the tops of the soaked pine trees gave an illusion that it was still raining lightly. Above the trees, the sun remained hidden behind the thick grey clouds, which looked only slightly more friendly than the ones that had heralded the coming of yesterday's storm.

Roy stopped and looked up at the ugly sky. "I wonder what time it is."

Mack stopped and propped his arm up against a tree. He had wanted to suggest they take a break, and Roy had given him the perfect opportunity. "Don't know," Mack said then he panted a few more breaths before he continued, "Probably around noon or a little after."

Mack had never been in the best of shape, and walking for almost two solid hours had really exhausted him. Noticing the flushed color of Mack's face, Roy had even begun to wonder if this walk might be a little much for Mack. He knew his boss was bad about not taking his blood pressure medicine.

"You okay?" Roy asked.

"Oh, hell yeah," Mack panted sarcastically. "Just wonderful."

"We ain't gonna have to carry you are we?" Harry asked with a grin.

"Screw you and the horse you rode in on." Mack replied, then he asked, "Are you sure we're headin' east, 'cause we sure should have hit the road by now?"

"We're goin' east all right." Harry replied, "I guarantee it, but..."

"But what?"

"Well, look at the trees." Harry said and motioned around him. "They're all huge like the ones we were cuttin' back at the site. I haven't heard of single place where you can find this many old trees, and you sure can't find 'em near a highway."

"So you're sayin' we're lost." Mack said.

"Naw, I'm just sayin' we're still not close to the highway. Probably got a ways to go yet."

"There's no damn way we were this far off the road," Roy added, as he looked around at the tall pines. "Are you *sure* we're headin' east."

"Yeah," Harry replied, but his tone didn't sound very confident.

Not liking the sound of that, Mack asked, "I thought you never got turned around in the woods."

"Well, this is east," Harry said, pointing in the direction they had been walking, "but I just can't figure out why we ain't found the road yet."

Mack took his arm from the tree, and straightened up, "We'd better get movin'."

"You sure you don't need to take a break?" Roy asked.

"I'll rest when I get to the house."

With that, they set off again, Harry still in the lead, with Mack behind him walking along holding his side. Roy walked a couple steps behind the other two, keeping a close eye on Mack.

They continued walking for a couple more minutes before Roy began to notice that it was considerably darker than it had been when they had taken their break.

"Is it getting darker?" Roy asked.

"No, you're just screwed in the head," Mack panted. "The story that boy told you's got you all worked up."

As they walked along, Roy began nervously glancing around. There was no doubt about it, the overcast darkness was rapidly giving way to twilight, but that was impossible. Wasn't it? The approaching darkness wasn't all that was bothering Roy. Like Derek, Roy had noticed that there didn't seem to be any creatures in the area. He hadn't seen the first squirrel or bird since they'd arrived. That had bothered him, but not near as much as the absence of crickets. It was very possible that he'd just missed seeing the birds and animals, but in this dark, wet weather the crickets should be out in force. And there was simply no way to miss their loud chirping. This also made Roy realize that he hadn't even swatted the first mosquito. The only thing that Roy had seen alive since yesterday were his coworkers and the big pine trees . . . and whatever that thing had been that he saw at his window last night.

"Let's head back," Roy blurted out.

"What?" Mack said as he stopped walking and turned around.

"Something's not right," Roy said.

"Yeah, your head's not screwed on right," Mack replied. "We can't be far from the road; it'd be stupid as hell to turn around now."

Mack started to add something else, but then he too noticed that it was rapidly getting dark. Thinking that the clouds had darkened in preparation for another shower, he tilted his head back and looked to the sky, but he found that it was already so dark that he could barely make out the tops of the trees, much less the clouds over them.

"The road can't be far," Harry said, with a slight tremor in his voice. He had also noticed the premature nightfall.

"Let's go then," Mack said, starting off in the direction they had been heading.

Harry started that way too, but Roy stayed put.

"I think we should turn back," Roy said.

Mack stopped and turned back to face him; in the darkness his face once again looked sincere. "We'll never get there in time, and the road can't be much farther. Besides, we'd never find it."

"I think we'd fare better lookin' for it that it than we would lookin' for the road."

"What do you mean?"

"I don't think the road's gonna be there no matter how far we walk."

Before Mack could reply, they were interrupted by the unmistakable sound of something moving off to the south of them (if Harry was right and they had been heading east, that is). Since they had been in the strange woods, they had seen very little underbrush, but about fifty feet to the south there seemed to be a long line of brush, probably running alongside a steam. A light rustling sound came from this brush, as if something were there walking along the creek, careful not to be seen, but obviously not very worried about being heard.

"Oh, hell," Harry muttered in broken voice that sounded like he was on the verge of tears.

"Probably just a deer," Mack whispered. "Tush hog at the worst, nothin' to go wettin' your drawers over."

The darkness continued to fall until only the upper outline of the brush was visible, then it disappeared altogether.

Behind Mack and Harry, Roy took a hesitant step away from the line of bushes. Then another.

Whatever was in the brush suddenly stopped moving. For a couple of minutes there was an uneasy silence, broken only by the steady dripping of raindrops from the tree limbs to the pinestraw below. Mack, Roy, and Harry stood in silence but couldn't hear any movement from the brush ahead. Then there was a sudden violent rustling, the unmistakable sound of something crashing towards them.

They turned and ran, but Harry only made it a couple of steps before a powerful blow to his back sent him sprawling face first onto the ground. There was no time for him to rise before whatever it was that had knocked him down was on top of him, ripping and tearing.

Roy and Mack ran away from the sound of Harry's screams, which continued for only a few seconds before they were silenced.

As Roy ran through the woods, he could hear Mack panting as he followed along not far behind. Roy's concern over his boss/friend's medical condition had been all but forgotten in the excitement, but when he heard Mack swear then fall to the ground, he immediately feared Mack was having a heart attack.

Roy stopped, but he didn't say a word or start back to where he had heard Mack fall. He was torn between helping Mack and continuing his flight. If Mack was having an attack, there wasn't anything he could do, but part of him couldn't help but want to return and try to help the man he'd worked with for over thirty years.

Nevertheless, Roy had almost convinced himself to press on without Mack, when he heard Mack called out in a part-whisper, part-shout, "Roy, I think I turned my ankle. Come give me a hand."

Roy didn't answer or return to help Mack, nor did he turn tail and run. He stayed put. A mental war was being fought in his head over which course of action to take.

"Roy!" Mack called out, this time in a little louder voice, "You out there? Come give me a hand."

"I'm comin'."

Roy started hesitantly back the way he'd come, "Where are you? Talk to me so I can locate you."

"Over here," Mack said, his voice lined heavily with fear. "I'm at the base of one of these monster pines. Damn near ran it. What the hell was that damn thing?"

Then Roy began to realize that he wasn't the only thing that could use Mack's voice to locate him. Whatever had gotten Harry could do the same. Suddenly Roy had wished he hadn't told Mack to talk. While Mack continued cussing about the darkness and the pines, Roy frantically ran toward the voice, hoping to get there and shut Mack up before something else did just that. When he could tell he was close, Roy told Mack to hush, that he could find him now. Understanding the situation, Mack quit talking in mid-sentence and didn't say another word. Roy walked on for another twenty feet or so before he practically stumbled over his boss in the dark.

"Right here," Mack said in a voice that was little more than a whisper.

"How bad?" Roy asked as he kneeled down but still keeping a constant lookout with his eyes.

"Bad enough. I don't think I'm gonna be able to put much weight on it, but if you help me up I might could get around a little."

Roy looked down at Mack, then looked back in the direction they'd come. He could see nor hear any movement. Perhaps whatever it was that had attacked them had stayed its pursuit. If it was some sort of bear, perhaps Harry had bought them some time by becoming the beast's meal.

Roy stood back up and extended his hand. Mack grasped Roy's hand at the wrist, and Roy grabbed Mack's hand likewise and gave a good pull.

Mack had just climbed to his feet, and hadn't even let go of Roy's hand, when it rushed them. Obviously, the creature, whatever it was, could be quite stealthy when it wanted to be. It had managed to sneak within around twenty feet of Roy and Mack without being noticed. When it surged forward a sound emitted from its throat that sounded part-growl, part-roar, and all evil. The sound had a deep quavering almost human sound to it. Roy turned, but in the darkness all he could see were red glowing eyes, and its mouth. Its mouth was partially opened in preparation of taking a good-sized bite out of either Roy or Mack; large carnivorous teeth were readily apparent. But what made the mouth so illuminant in the darkness was the flames that were jumping from the creature's throat and licking upward past its lips.

Roy turned to run, but Mack didn't let go of his hand. Roy couldn't break free.

The creature slammed into Mack, driving him back into the tree. The force of the impact also knocked Roy to the ground and freed him of Mack's grip. From where he'd fallen, Roy saw Mack pinned with his back to the tree by something large. Other than those terrible eyes and its flaming mouth, Roy could only make out the outline of the creature in the darkness. The massive beast was standing on two legs, pinning Mack to the tree with its arms. It was hunkered down so that its face was even with Mack's, but Roy could tell from its outline that if it stood up straight it would stand at least eight feet tall, probably more like nine. Its face seemed to resemble that of an enormous dog.

It slowly moved its face closer to Mack's.

Mack screamed.

In one swift motion, the creature turned his head sideways and snapped its jaws on either side of Mack's head. It bit and twisted its head sharply, tearing Mack's head completely from his body.

Roy scrambled to his feet and fled, running blindly through the woods. He ran in no particular direction, just away from that terrible beast. He continued to run for some time, never venturing a glance back, for fear of what he'd see. Several times he heard, or imagined he heard, the terrible sound that the beast had made as it rushed them, each time he would let out a startled cry and try to run faster, which was impossible—he was already running as fast as his legs could possibly carry him.

Since he was running without taking glances over his shoulder, watching only for pine trees that might get in his way, it was quite odd that he literally tripped over the front porch of the old cabin without ever seeing it. Of course the irony didn't dawn on Roy, who was crying and babbling incoherently when Derek and Kevin came out on the porch, picked him up, and carried him inside.

—Thirteen—

I'M TELLIN' YOU IT WAS RIGHT HERE," Don said, pointing at a place in the edge of the woods where there was definitely no road.

Deputy Alex Smith shifted his weight from one leg to the other and covered his mouth to muffle a mock cough—the real reason he brought his hand to his face was to cover his smile. He had been called out on some wild ones before, but a disappearing logging crew that drove down a road that wasn't there any more? This had to be the tops.

After pointing the place out to the deputy for the fourth time, Don stood staring at the edge of the woods like he thought if he looked hard enough the road would magically reappear. Don looked rough. He hadn't shaved, and his eyes were baggy and bloodshot. He'd only had thirty minutes of sleep last night, if that.

Sue stood just behind the officer, wringing her hands before her. The little woman had had even less sleep the night before, none at all, and she looked every bit as rough as Don. Roy's plump little wife had never been what one would call attractive, but without her makeup and without any sleep for over twenty-four hours, she was downright scary.

"I don't know what to say, Mr. Elkins," Deputy Smith finally said, finally bringing his hand down from his mouth now that he felt he could keep a straight face. "Are you positive that we're not in the wrong place?"

"I've already told you," Don said, now becoming visibly agitated, "I've looked up and down this road all yesterday and all last night, this is the place. I know it is. I remember that creek." Don said pointing back at the little stream, "and I remember that I could just see the Berryman's mailbox up ahead." Don then turned and pointed the other direction down the road.

"Well, it's been twenty-four hours, so we can go back to the sheriff's office and fill out a missing persons form if you want to."

"There's nothing else you can do?" Sue asked.

The first thought that popped to Deputy Smith's head was replying that they could put out an APB on a missing dirt road. This caused him to suddenly need his hand over his mouth for yet another phantom cough. "Uh, no ma'am. I'm afraid that's all I can do right now."

Don continued staring blankly at the woods for a couple more seconds, then he said, "Let's go fill out those papers then."

* * *

They had been on the porch since the first rays of daylight broke through the treetops. They stood in silence, watching as the sun lazily rose higher into the sky. After what seemed to be an hour—of course, there was no way to tell for sure how long it had been; time didn't seem to be functioning properly anymore—Kevin finally turned to Derek and spoke.

"What do we do now?"

Derek just shrugged.

As far as Derek and Kevin could tell, there had been no creature stalking around the cabin last night. Neither of them had heard a single thing until Roy's collision with the porch aroused them from their troubled sleep.

Roy was in bad shape. Obviously in shock, he alternated between babbling about a fire-breathing bear eating Mack and Harry, crying and sobbing, and laughing hysterically. The boys had placed him on the bed, and tried to get him to lie down, but he wouldn't cooperate. He sat on the edge of the bed going through the three phases of his alternating emotions. It was quite some time before he calmed down enough for the boys to make any sense of his ramblings. Apparently when the three men had tried to walk out of the woods, the darkness had fallen much sooner than they had expected. Not long after night fell, the three men were attacked something huge; it resembled a nine-foot tall cross between a dog, a bear, and a man. It had killed Harry, then Mack, but Roy had managed to get away and somehow stumble on the cabin in the dark.

After several hours, Roy finally fell asleep. His sleep was strongly induced by physical and emotional exhaustion. He didn't really calm down and fall asleep; he passed out.

Derek and Kevin stood in silence for a little while longer, before

Derek answered Kevin's question, "I guess we could walk back to the truck and see if anything will crank."

"I doubt that very seriously."

"Well, what do you want to do, sit and wait here?" Derek replied, with a hint of agitation apparent in his voice, "What's it going to hurt to go try?"

"How do we know it's not going to turn dark on us like it did on Mack and them?"

"It's only a couple hundred yards."

"It's supposedly only a mile or two to the road, but Mack and them walked for hours without ever seeing the road."

"Damn it, Kevin, we can't just sit here!"

"Calm down, man," Kevin said, then he turned and walked back to the cabin's door. Scratching his head and thinking. He then propped both hands on the door, like a criminal about to be frisked, and hung his head down between his arms. "I guess we could give it a go. The way things look, nobody's going to be able to find us . . . wherever the hell we are."

"Do you think we ought to tell Roy? I know he's not going to want to go, but he might freak out again when we tell him where we're going.

"We need to tell him. He won't freak half as bad as he would waking up and finding us gone."

"Good point," Derek said; then he turned away from the woods and toward the door, "Well, let's get it over with."

Inside, they found Roy awake, but he didn't quite seem all there. He was sitting on the edge of the bed, staring blankly off into space. His face looked considerably older. His jaw was slack, and his mouth was open enough to enable the boys to tell he'd taken out his teeth, but not enough to expose his gums. His eyes were baggy, and the lines in his face seemed to have deepened overnight. Roy had been in no condition to shave this morning, even if he did have a good razor, which he didn't. The whiskers that had grown in were grey, almost white, on the upper part of his cheeks and on his chin. The stark contrast between these whiskers and his black hair and dark complexioned skin added to the effect, making the fifty-seven year old man look every bit of one hundred years old.

"Hey, Roy?" Derek said softly as he approached.

Roy blinked once, as if waking or snapping out of a hypnotist's trance, then he looked over at Derek without saying a word. His eyes seemed only semi-focused.

"Me and Kevin are gonna go see if we can get any of the equipment to start. We'll be right back."

At first Roy didn't reply. He continued staring at Derek almost as if he was trying to figure out who he was, then he smacked his gums—an action that made him look even older—and said in a surprisingly calm voice, "I don't know if that's such a good idea."

"We'll be right back," Kevin added, "And if it starts looking like it's getting dark, while we're on the way we'll turn right around."

Roy slowly shook his head. "It don't matter. If that thing wants you, he'll get you. He'll stretch the distance between wherever you are and the cabin so that you can't make it back, then he'll snuff out the sun and come for you. I . . . I think we're safe here . . . for now."

Kevin glanced over at Derek, and for a second Derek thought his friend was going to side with Roy. But he didn't.

"Let's go," Kevin said. "He'll be okay."

Derek nodded, then turned back to Roy. "We're going Roy. We'll be right back."

Without a word, Roy turned his head away from Derek and back toward the wall.

* * *

When the boys reached the top of the slope, the first thing they noticed was that the fallen tree that Kevin had cut down was no longer there. They hurried past where the tree had lain, and didn't stand around long enough to find the stump, but they were both sure that they would find that there was a tall tree standing where the stump had once been.

When they came into the area where they had left the equipment, they were in for another shock. All three vehicles were completely rusted out. With its thinner body, the pickup was worst of the lot. It was one solid reddish rust color, with several holes all along the hood and the fenders where the rust had eaten through. The pickup's tires had rotted and gone flat, and there was even a small tree that was growing in from the floorboard and passing out the broken driver's side window. The rusted out skidder looked like some sort of lame four-legged monster, with its massive tires now flat and its body riding much lower to the ground than it should have. The dozer looked the best out of the three, but it only took a passing glance to tell that it was now absolutely worthless. Aside from several other less obvious problems, the left tread had rusted to the point that it had fallen off.

The boys walked silently past Mack's pickup until they were roughly in the center of the four vehicles, where the few logs that Roy had managed to drag up before the skidder quit were supposed to be. There wasn't a single log in sight, not one that wasn't vertical and still attached to a tree anyway.

"Son of a bitch," Kevin gasped, finally breaking the silence.

"Yeah," Derek muttered. At the time, this was all he could think of in the way of a reply.

"So much for finding something that works," Kevin said in a hushed voice.

Then he turned his head to the sky to make sure the sun wasn't trying to sneak its way out of the sky. Seeing Kevin look up, Derek quickly jerked his head upwards, fully expecting to see the sun making a beeline for the western horizon. But the sun still stood over in the east.

"I guess we might as well head back," Kevin said. "There's no use even trying these engines."

"There might be something else useful, though."

"Like what?" Kevin asked, but Derek had already set off toward the pickup.

Derek rummaged through the back of the pickup but couldn't find a single thing that could be of use. He found Roy's toolbox, but what good would an extensive set of rusted wrenches do them now? If there were any carpenter's tools it might be another story, but there weren't any in Mack's truck. There were all sorts of chainsaw equipment, but all of it was now worthless. There was even an axehead, but the handle had rotted off, making it useless. And there certainly wasn't anything in the way of food in the pickup.

Derek was just about to give up when he spied something that had almost slipped through one of the rust holes in the truck bed. It was an old, and extremely rusted, machete. The rubber handle was brittle, but it was still functional.

Derek smiled, then picked the machete up and held it over his head triumphantly, like King Arthur having just pulled Excalibur from the stone.

"It's probably too rusted to be any good," Kevin said.

Derek bent the blade slightly, to see if it was rusted through and through. If it was, it would snap in two without applying much pressure. The blade held.

"It's still too rusty. It won't have an edge."

"Damn it, quit your belly-achin'," Derek said as he ran the blade across his forearm, it left a reddish-brown line of rust, but didn't even come close to breaking the skin, "Well, it may not be sharp, but the blade's narrow enough that if I swing it hard enough, it'll cut whatever I hit. That or knock the hell out of it, either way's fine with me."

Derek then turned back to the pickup; he had given himself an idea. He rummaged through Roy's toolbox until he came to a heavy iron wrench. It was only about a foot long, but it weighed a good ten pounds -- definitely capable of knocking the hell out of something.

Derek took the wrench out and handed it to Kevin. "Now we're armed."

Kevin looked over the rusted tool. It was obvious that Derek felt much better now that he had found the machete and the wrench, but Kevin didn't feel the least bit better off holding what he considered a worthless hunk of metal that would only serve as an effective club if the ten foot bear, or whatever it was, was kind enough to sit still while Kevin walked right up to it and took a good swing.

Not only that, but they still hadn't found anything to eat, and, judging by the lack of wildlife in the woods, it was doubtful they were going find anything. It was small consolation to know that there was a thin chance that they could fend off whatever it was that was attacking them long enough to die of starvation rather than its terrible claws.

—Fourteen—

THAT NIGHT THE CREATURE became bolder. It tromped heavily around the house, often stopping at the door to the cabin. Once the creature even pushed the door open about an inch, as it had in Mr. Kinney's story. Roy sobbed uncontrollably the whole time the creature made its way around the house, and when it began slowly opening the door, it was more than he could handle. He huddled down between the bed and the far wall and began screaming at the top of his lungs. With Roy's shrieks ringing in their ears, Kevin and Derek surged for the door and tried to shut it. At first they couldn't make it budge; the door remained open about one inch, not opening any further, but not shutting either. Finally, using every once of strength in their bodies, Kevin and Derek were able to little by little force the door shut. The creature continued applying pressure to the door for a couple more minutes, then it just stood there. For about ten minutes no more footsteps were heard, then the creature tromped off the porch and back onto the pinestraw littered ground.

The creature came once more that night, not long before sunrise. It made one circle around the cabin, sending Roy into another fit of hysterics, then it went away and didn't come back. That night, anyway.

The next day was spent trying to care of Roy, who had by now quite thoroughly lost his mind. He ranted and raved for a while, then he would sit and quietly sulk. He stayed in the corner between the bed and the wall, and Kevin and Derek's best efforts were unable to convince him to come out. And if he wasn't coming out from behind the bed, it was certainly too much to ask for him to go outside when nature called. Twice during the day Roy unzipped his fly and pissed on the floor. And it got worse. Toward the end of the day, during his rantings, Roy started repeatedly mentioning his stomach hurting. Not long after he quit complaining, a terrible odor filled the room and it became apparent that Roy had crapped in his pants. Kevin and Derek attempted to convince Roy to give him his pants so they could take them outside and wash them as best they could, but he wouldn't go for it. The smell was too much; something had to be done. The boys attempted to take the pants by force, but when they did, they were introduced first hand to the old saying about a madman having the strength of several men. Just when it seemed they where going to have to put up with the smell all night, Roy had a brief moment of clarity. Without a word, he shucked his pants and his underdrawers, walked to the door and threw them in the yard, then he walked back to his little hiding place and began sobbing that he was sorry.

In a few minutes, Roy was ranting again.

As soon as night fell, the creature made its appearance. They heard it first at the back of the cabin, then it made its way to the front. This time it didn't walk circles around the cabin. It went straight to the door and started slowly opening it. Kevin and Derek had prepared for this, like Mr. Kinney, they had moved the bed over to the door, but they had also taken several heavy items from the vehicles, and made a sort of barricade. They were sure that the combined weight of all the rusty tools, equipment, and even engine parts, as well as their own strength and weight, would be enough to stop whatever was out there from being able to budge the door, but as soon as the creature began to push the mass of rusty metal that had been piled on the inside began to give way. For what seemed like eternity, the boys struggled to keep the door shut. The whole time they struggled, the door never opened more than two inches or closed to less that a half an inch.

During this time Roy was strangely silent. Naked from the waist down, he sat on the floor in the far corner, watching the struggle with detached interest. When the creature finally quit its assault on the door some time in the middle of the night, Roy's gaze shifted slowly away from the door to a blank spot on the wall.

"Ain't no use," Roy said as soon as the boys began replacing the barrier, his voice surprisingly calm. "It's gonna get us, just like it got Mack and Harry."

"Don't talk like that, Roy," Derek said as he slid one of the rusty chainsaws against the door.

Moving slowly and awkwardly, like a feeble old man, Roy got to his feet.

"Give us a hand here," Kevin said as he attempted to heave the skidder's old rusty claw onto the top of the pile before the door.

"I want to go out."

All work in the room ceased. The claw Kevin had been lifting slipped from his grip before it was in place and crashed to the floor, taking part of the barrier with it.

"You can't go out there," Derek said.

"Might as well. It's gonna be in here soon enough. Why not get it over with?"

"We've held it off for two nights," Kevin said. "What makes you think we can't keep it up until help comes? Hell, now that you're up, there's three of us. The odds are that much better."

"Can't you see? It's playing with you like a cat playing with a mouse. It could come through that door whenever it wanted to."

At first no one replied, then Derek half-heartedly muttered, "Bullshit."

"We're as good as dead in here," Roy said, his voice becoming shaky and less stable as he spoke. "We might as well get it over."

"Don't be ridiculous," Kevin said.

"I'm going out," Roy said, his body beginning to tremble.

"No, you're not," Derek said sternly.

"I'm going out," Roy repeated, his eyes becoming wild, froth appearing in the corners of his mouth as his voice rose to a scream, *"I'm going out! I'm going out! I'M GOING OUT!"*

"Oh, hell," Kevin murmured.

Roy launched himself past the boys and frantically began removing objects from the barricade. Kevin and Derek tried to pull Roy away and Derek was rewarded with an elbow to the mouth that sent him to the floor. Next, Kevin was shoved into the pantry. He recovered quickly, then came at Roy with his heavy wrench held high, hoping to knock Roy unconscious or at least stun him. But Roy proved quite fast and agile; he deflected the blow with his left hand, then popped Kevin in the nose with his right. The rusty wrench fell to the floor, followed by Kevin. Exhausted from their earlier battle with the creature, this was all the resistance Kevin and Derek could muster.

Roy began laughing hysterically as he removed the last of the barricade and his voice rose to a wild cackle as he bounded out the door. No sooner had he left the boys' sight than the laughter abruptly stopped—the creature had been waiting right outside the door. There was no screaming or begging for mercy, just a wet thump, then silence.

Kevin and Derek stared at the wide open door, expecting their demon to lumber out of the shadows and into the cabin to finish them off, but it didn't. After five long minutes they heard heavy footfalls moving away from the cabin and into the woods.

Derek slowly got up from the cabin's wooden floor and shut the door. They made no effort to replace the barrier.

—Fifteen—

DON KNEW WHO IT WAS as soon as the phone rang. Over the last two days Don had either been with Sue or talking to her on the phone, inevitably trying to console her, no matter the form of communication. Three of Don's best friends were missing, but one of those men was poor Sue Laviolette's husband.

Stupid jumped from the pillow beside Don's head and began yapping at the phone as it rang away on the nightstand.

Don yawned, stretched and opened his weary eyes. The clock on the wall declared it was half past ten. Don had been up late talking to Sue, and, since he now was without a job, Don had slept well into the day.

"Hush," Don said, batting at the yapping poodle.

Taking this halfhearted swat as a sign that Don wanted to play, Stupid's barking changed to playful growls, which were just as quickly switched back to rapid fire yapping when the phone rang again.

Don picked up the phone. "Hello?"

"I may have found something," Sue blurted out. This was a change; she was usually bawling her eyes out.

Don quickly sat upright in bed. "What?"

Stupid was still yapping away and when another gentle swat didn't work, Don found Stupid Jr. among the sheets and threw the stuffed bear across the room.

"I went back to the Tax Office this morning and got Liz to let me look through the old property files. I found out who owned the land before Temple."

This *was* news. Yesterday morning Don and Sue had found out that the land was owned by Temple Inland, a large lumber corporation that was by far the biggest landowner in Sabine County. Don had then contacted Temple's main office to see if there was any cutting scheduled in the Southern portion of the county—there wasn't. Apparently whoever contacted Mack didn't own the land. This man had either forged his papers, or Mack had pulled one of his drunken stunts and had forgotten to ask. The property ownership had proved a dead end. However, maybe the previous owner might know something.

Sue continued, "His name is Dalton Alford. I did a little calling around and found out that Mr. Alford is in the nursing home here in town."

Don swung his legs out of the bed and began searching for his pants. "I'll come by and pick you up."

* * *

"Kevin, wake up. I've got an idea."

Kevin stirred from his makeshift bed, which consisted of the quilt stretched out on the floor and the pillow—the cabin's usual bed was currently buried under the rusty iron tools and engine that made up the barrier behind the door. His eyes blinked twice as they tried to focus, then he grimaced in pain as he shifted position; his back was in knots from sleeping on the hard floor. It was a toss up as to which hurt the worse, his nose or his back.

"I think I know how we can get out of here," Derek said once he was sure Kevin was fully awake.

"How?" Kevin asked.

"We'll build a fire—a big one. The wind is calm so the smoke will travel up above the trees. Someone's bound to be looking for us; when they see the smoke they'll be able follow it to the cabin."

Kevin took a long hard look at Derek. Despite the bags under his eyes and his swollen chin, Derek actually looked excited—he actually believed this plan would work. Kevin, on the other hand, did not. "It won't work," he said, flatly.

"Why not?"

"For one thing, I don't think anyone would see the smoke if we set the whole woods on fire."

"What do you mean?"

Kevin barked out a brief, borderline hysterical laugh and said, "I'm not sure if we're in Oz, Mars, or Hell, but, Toto, I don't think we're in Texas anymore."

Derek shook his head. "I didn't see a tornado, did you? There's definitely something wrong with this place, but we got here, that means someone else can. Sure, time and distance seems to be a little out of whack, but a pillar of smoke can be seen from a long way off. And if someone's already missing, then they'll send help immediately."

"Okay, let's just say that someone does see our smoke. What then? Are they going to have any better luck getting out of here?"

"If they're in a helicopter, hell yeah."

"Oh, come on. Think about what you're saying," Kevin said as he rose to his feet. "Someone gets lost in these woods at least twice a year. When's the last time you remember them searching with a helicopter? If help comes, it'll be in the form of two or three forest rangers on foot—horseback at best."

"Hey, if help comes and they can't get us out, then the more the merrier. We'd definitely be able to hold the door with a few more hands. And you can bet your ass that if two or three forest rangers go missing, those rescue helicopters would be circling the area within twenty-four hours."

Kevin rubbed his stomach, then grumbled, "Well I hope your saviors show up with some grub. If not, this is going to turn into the Dahmer Party real quick."

Derek managed a smile despite the stress of the situation and said, "It's Donner Party, college boy. I think you're getting your cannibals confused."

"Whatever."

Derek's voice turned serious. "Look, Kevin, you can curl up and die if you want to, but don't expect me to lie down beside you." Derek turned and started toward the door.

"Where are you going?"

"Outside," Derek replied over his shoulder. "There's no telling how much daylight we'll have today, if I'm going to build that fire I'd better get started."

Kevin sighed heavily, then followed Derek outside.

* * *

The first rays of sunlight were breaking through the trees and in the sky the deep blue of dawn had yet to give way to the fair blue of broad daylight. It was still morning, and time seemed to be passing somewhat normally . . . so far.

Derek stood looking up at one of the enormous trees right outside the cabin. "Well, we've got enough timber, just no way to bring it down. We'll have to use underbrush, pinestraw, low hanging limbs, and the furniture in the cabin." Derek took lowered his eyes from the heavens, turned to Kevin, and began laying out his plan. "We can also make a trip to the vehicles to get tires and anything else we can find that'll burn. Once we get back, we need to stay within sight of the cabin. It seems time and distance are both screwed up here. Time we can't do a thing about, but if we stay within sight of the cabin I don't think the distance will change."

Dozens of objections to Derek's plan popped to Kevin's mind, but he held his tongue. In fact, some of Derek's enthusiasm for the plan was beginning to rub off on him. He began to feel as if this plan just might work.

"Let's get started," Derek said. He headed off in the direction of the vehicles with Kevin right behind him.

At the vehicles the boys found very little that would be off any use. The tires were now so rotten that very little rubber remained. Most of the gas cans were of no use since they had rusted through and leaked their contents onto the ground. Only Harry's plastic gas can remained, and, judging by the weak smell of the gasoline inside, it was doubtful that its contents would be much help. This questionable container of gasoline, a few strips of rotten cloth from the interior of Mack's pickup, and a few brittle chunks of rubber from the skidder's tires were all the boys were able to find. The good news was the sun didn't make a beeline for the western horizon while the boys were away from the cabin. The trip took barely a half an hour, and, judging by the morning sun still parting the trees from the east, a half an hour was all that had passed.

"Now for the fun part," Derek said as he set his load down in front of the cabin. He drew his rusty machete from his belt. "I'll start chopping some low level limbs and seeing if I can find some fallen branches, and you try to start the fire using paper from the cabin and pinestraw. Get the pinestraw from under the porch; it'll be drier."

"Why don't I look for limbs and you start the fire," Kevin suggested. "You've got more experience with that sort of thing."

"Good idea," Derek said. He grasped the machete by its rusty blade and handed it to Kevin handle first. "Better get started."

After gathering a few twigs from around the cabin and as much semi-dry pinestraw as could be obtained from under the porch, Derek started trying to use the sparks from his lighter to light one of the pieces of paper from inside the cabin. The gas from Harry's can proved to be no good. In fact, Derek found that it actually dampened the paper like water, rendering it useless. Finally, after several missed attempts, Derek finally was able to start a tiny flame on the corner of one of the remaining dry sheets of paper. He placed this paper under the pile of twigs and began adding pinestraw. Slowly but surely the fire grew.

"We're in business!" Derek called out, "Hurry up with that wood!"

Kevin, who had just whacked the base of a sapling and was about to haul it back to the cabin, turned and called back, "I am hurrying! What do you think I am, a logger?"

Derek laughed.

Kevin was having considerable difficulty coming up with any wood for the fire. Low-lying limbs simply didn't exist on these tall pines and only a handful of younger trees and saplings existed among the monstrosities. Even fallen limbs were rare, as if the perfection of this timeless forest prevented the trees from even losing a portion of their being.

Kevin dragged his prize down the slope toward the fire.

Derek saw him coming. "Is that it?"

"There's not much out there, Derek," Kevin replied. "You might as well start breaking up the furniture, because that's about all we're going to find."

Derek turned back to the fire and motioned to a pair of thick wooden rods that had until recently been the legs of the table. "Already started. Once I get it going, I'll throw the mattress and the quilt on. It'll burn hot and give us lots of smoke for a little while, but it'll also burn quick. Keep trying to find some wood."

"I think I saw a fallen limb up the slope behind the cabin," Kevin said as he placed his sapling near the fire.

Behind the cabin Kevin found the limb. It was a thin branch, barely three feet long. Soaked but not waterlogged, the limb was better than nothing, but it certainly wasn't something that was going to bring their tiny flame to a blazing bonfire. Further investigation of the slope behind the cabin turned up three more damp limbs, the longest of which was two feet long.

"Hurry up!" Derek called out.

Kevin, who was at the top of the slope, cupped his hands to his mouth and called back. "I don't have much!"

"Bring it anyway! I'm almost out of furniture!"

Already? Kevin thought. His first impression was that time had given him a jump while he was collecting limbs, but he knew the simple fact was they didn't have enough dry wood. One chair, one table and one bed frame just wasn't going to be enough.

Still, they had to try.

With his small load of four damp limbs in his arms, Kevin ran down the hill toward the cabin. He could see a tiny pillar of smoke risking from the other side of the cabin where Derek was doing the best he could with what he had at hand. Maybe once the mattress was added the smoke would be thick enough to be seen from a distance; of course it wouldn't last, but it was their best hope.

Derek was removing the boards from the top of the table when Kevin rounded the corner. The chair was already gone and most of the bed frame was currently in the fire. Kevin trotted up and placed his load next to the fire.

"That's it?" Derek said, glancing at the four lonely branches.

Kevin didn't reply to Derek's comment. Watching Derek disassemble the table had given him an idea. "What about the cabin? It's made of wood?"

"Burn down the cabin? Are you crazy? It's all that's keeping that thing away from us at night."

"Not the whole cabin, just some of the outside boards," Kevin said, his heart leaping in his chest as he realized that his plan might very well be the much-needed solution to their problem. "We can take the boards off the porch. The porch's roof will have protected them from the weather. They'll be dry."

Derek rose up from his fire and glanced over at the cabin. "Hell, yeah. Get to it."

Kevin ran over to the cabin, grasped the edge of a board where it hung over the side of the porch, and tugged for all he was worth. With considerable straining, the nails began to give way with a loud creak not unlike a rusty hinge. Using the first board as a pry bar, the next half dozen boards came much easier. Once added to the fire, these boards had an immediate effect—the fire began blazing away. Since the fire no longer needed to be tended, Derek joined Kevin and soon all the planks halfway across the front of the porch were removed and in the fire.

On his way back to the porch from depositing an armload of boards onto the fire, Kevin turned back around and took a moment to admire their work. Orange tongues of flame were lapping skyward, spitting forth a heavy column of smoke that rose well above the tops of the tall trees.

"See if those shelves in the cabin will come off," Derek said from behind him.

"All right," Kevin said. He tore his gaze from their distress beacon and started into the cabin.

What Kevin saw inside stopped him cold.

At first he couldn't catch his breath to speak, then he managed to shout, "Derek! Come here!"

Derek dropped his armload of wood and sprinted over to where Kevin stood in the open cabin door. "Holy shit," Derek gasped.

Inside, the cabin was exactly as they had first found it. All of the furniture that they had so recently tossed to the fire was present. The table, chair, and bed were sitting exactly were they first found them. The rusty equipment and tools were gone, and even the boys' muddy footprints were gone. It appeared as if a team of maids had just given the place a cleaning that could pass a white glove inspection.

A sinking feeling filled both boys' chests, and they slowly turned their heads back to the yard. Sure enough, all the boards were back in place on the porch and the fire was out. In fact, it appeared as if the fire had never been there in the first place since there wasn't even a black spot in the pinestraw to mark its location.

Worse yet, the sky was darkening as night was making its sudden appearance.

—Sixteen—

FROM OUTSIDE THE Shady Grove Nursing Home appeared clean and tranquil. The grand entrance appeared similar to that of an old Southern plantation. The rest of the rustic brick building, as well as the immaculately landscaped yard, was designed in perfect symmetry around this stately entrance. Just to the right of the front door, a pair of elderly gentlemen sat on a park bench playing a game of checkers. Don recognized one of the men as Holt Tubbins, an old logging hand who had worked with his father.

"Morning, Holt," Don said with a smile, his hand extended. "Long time no see."

Sue, who had been walking briskly ahead of Don, came to a halt at the door.

Holt turned to Don, his eyes squinted and his cheeks reddened as the rusty gears began turning.

"Don," Don said helpfully, "Don Elkins. Carl Elkins's son."

"Huh?"

"You'll have to speak up," the skinny old man across for Holt said, "He can't hear worth a shit."

Don raised his voice, "Don Elkins. Carl's boy."

Slowly recognition appeared on the old logger's face. He took Don's hand. "Well I'll be damn," Holt trumpeted in a loud voice that certainly suggested his hearing was exactly top notch. "Well, I'll be. How's the world been treatin' you, Carl?"

"No, Don, not Carl," Don replied, "I'm Carl's middle son."

"Yeah, I remember ole Don. How is the boy?"

"No, *I'm* Don. Carl died back in eighty-eight."

"No shit?" Holt said. He ran one of his big hands over his bald scalp and Don suddenly realized this was a throwback from an old habit Holt used to have of running his fingers through his thick greasy hair. "How'd it happen? Loggin' accident?"

"No, sir. Cancer got him."

"Huh?"

"Cancer," Don said at a volume just this side of yelling, "He got sick."

"Damn, that's a shame. What about your other two boys, they doin' all right," Holt replied, obviously still believing Don was Carl.

"Are you coming?" Sue said, her normally sheepish voice having a bit of an edge.

"Uh, yeah," Don said to Sue in a normal voice. He turned back to Holt and belted out, "I'll see you around."

"Okay, good to see you."

Don turned and followed Sue into the nursing home.

Once through the grand entrance and past the elegant lobby, Don found the rest of the nursing home entirely different. The interior was designed exactly like a hospital, with a nurses' station directly before the entrance and rooms extending down a pair of halls extending to the left and right. The only decorations were a few scattered portraits along the walls, a solitary potted plant resting on the counter of the nurses' station, and an oversized event calendar. A rickety old housekeeping cart was positioned beside the station, overflowing with laundry. A hunched old woman with a walker was making her way across the room at an impossibly slow pace, mumbling to herself as she inched along. To the left of the station, a frail old black man with a cane was staring blankly at an empty space of wall. An enormously obese old man was behind him in a wheelchair, constantly tugging at the long tail of his sleeping gown like a small child tugging on Mommy's dress to tell her he has to go potty right now. Across from these two, an old woman in a hospital gown was screaming at the top of her lungs while she used her cane to ward off imaginary pigs that her long-dead husband had carelessly let out of their pen.

"Git them damn hawgs back in that pen!" the woman shrieked. "Judd, damn it, I told ya to keep that gate locked! That new sow done figured out how ta open the gate!"

Don was somewhat startled by all this; he paused, taking it all in. But not Sue. She trooped right up to the nurses' station like a woman on a mission that had been handed her straight from the Almighty.

An anorexic-thin late-to-middle-aged woman was behind the nurses' station filling out a medical chart. If it hadn't been for her white uniform and the fact she was behind the counter, she probably would have been mistaken for one of elderly residents of the home. Her frail arms and wrinkled face certainly made her appear as though she belonged here on a permanent basis.

"I'm here to speak to one of you patients," Sue told the woman.

The nurse didn't so much as look up.

"Excuse me," Sue said, "We're here to see Dalton Alford."

"One second," the nurse replied sharply, still without looking up.

Sue stood impatiently in front of the desk, her hands in constant motion, wringing a damp handkerchief she'd been using to dab her tears. The nurse kept them waiting for no longer than thirty seconds, but this was much to long for Sue.

"Excuse me, but . . ." Sue began.

The nurse turned her attention from the chart to address a nurses' aid who had just entered the nurses' station behind her. "Barbara, do you think you could help these people?" the thin nurse said sharply.

"Sho can," Barbara replied, then she waddled her way back out of the nurses' station and over to where Sue and Don were standing. A wide, exceedingly cheerful smile stretched across the obese lady's round ebony face—she looked like an overgrown black cherub. "Can I hep you?"

"We're here to see Mr. Dalton Alford," Sue said.

"Right dis way," the round cherub said, then she turned and waddled down the hall to the right.

Once Sue had started after Barbara, Don turned to the old nurse behind the counter. "Ma'am, I'm sorry if Sue seemed a little rude. She's just a little worked up."

Once again the nurse never looked up or uttered a word.

Don turned and hurried after Barbara and Sue.

"You have to excuse Wilma," Barbara was saying. "That woman old enough to be past her monthly, but I think she gonna bleed to death." Barbara stopped and turned to Sue and Don, her face still glowing cheerfully, "Now don't you go an' tell her I said that."

"We won't," Don said.

Barbara laughed, her entire body trembling as she did so. "I know you won't, honey." The big woman turned and resumed her trek down the hall, still chuckling.

They passed by a couple more doors before Barbara turned into a room to her left. Unsure of whether to follow or stay in the hall, Sue and Don stood in the doorway. They could make out the foot of a pair of beds in the room.

"How you dis mornin' Missa Alford?" Barbara said, addressing the resident in the first bed.

"Barbara?" a frail, hoarse voice answered.

"Das right," Barbara replied, drawing the curtain that separated the two beds.

"How's my sweetheart today?"

Barbara rolled out a round of jolly laughter, then said, "Couldn't be better. Got you a couple visitors today."

"Not that damn preacher man and his wife is it?"

"No, suh. Didn't say who they is."

"Well they ain't my family, that's for damn sure," the hoarse voice said. "They know I don't have a dime to my name."

Barbara turned to the door and saw Don and Sue standing in the doorway. "Come on in," she said, her face still glowing.

Don and Sue shuffled on into the room.

"Jus holler if you need me," Barbara said, making her way out the door.

Dalton Alford was a wretched sight to behold. The thin sheet revealed his body to be little more than a layer of skin stretched across a bone frame. His deep eye sockets and wrinkled cheeks were hollow and his toothless mouth was sunken and drawn. A thin plastic tube ran under his nose, with a pair of prongs jabbing upwards into the nostrils themselves; the other end of the tube was attached to a large green oxygen bottle resting beside the bed. A plastic bag filled with a dirty orangeish fluid was attached to the lower part of his bed; a tube ran from this bag up under the sheet—a catheter.

"Sweet gal, that Barbara," Dalton Alford said hoarsely.

"She seems it," Don commented.

Mr. Alford's cloudy eyes stared off into space; he was quite obviously blind. Still, he turned his head in the vague direction of Don's voice. "Well, are ya'll gonna introduce yourselves or just stand there?"

"I'm Don Elkins, and this here is Sue Laviolette."

"You any kin to Tom Elkins?"

"That's my uncle," Don said, "My father was Carl."

"I hope to hell your daddy was a better man than his brother," Mr. Alford said. He took a couple of deep breaths through his nose before continuing. "Tom Elkins was one worthless son of a bitch."

"Oh," Don said, somewhat caught off guard by the old man's bluntness.

"No offence," Mr. Alford said after a few moments of silence.

"No, none taken."

"Well, what can I do for you?"

"Uh, we need to ask you a few questions," Don said, stepping up to the edge of the bed. "It's about some land you used to own."

"You can stop right there, mister," Mr. Alford, lifting his hand ever so slowly, as if it took a great amount of effort. "If you're trying to get an old man into some illegal logging scheme, let me tell you right now, that shit ain't gonna fly. I've been down that road before." He took another deep breath on his machine, then continued, "It must be something in the blood, 'cause your damn uncle was the same way."

"No, sir," Don said, "this don't have anything to do with logging." Then Don paused, actually it did have something to do with logging.

"Well, what the hell do you want then?"

Injured family pride combined with frustration over the fact that this decrepit old goat was completely dominating the conversation to give Don a sudden surge of hatred for the old man in the bed before him. Don had been through a lot over the last couple of days. He was usually not the type of man prone to violence, but he was now finding himself fighting the urge to grab this man by the shoulders and give him a good shaking. The only thread holding Don's temper at bay was the simple fact that if he did shake this little old man, he would probably break him.

"I just need to ask a few questions about some land you own," Don said in a slow measured voice.

"Don't own any land," the old man said, "Sold it all before moving here."

Don gritted his teeth, "*Used to own*. I want to talk you about some land you *used to own*."

Mr. Alford took another long wheezy breath on his nasal tube before saying, "If you've got a problem with some land that used to be mine you need to take it up with whoever owns it now. Sold most of it to Temple."

"No, I . . ." Don started, his voice rising in anger but he was interrupted.

"Mr. Alford," Sue said, her quavering as if she was on the verge of tears, yet still having a definite edge of steel. "My husband and four other men have gone missing. I . . . I think something terrible may have happened to them."

"Missing?" Mr. Alford said, suddenly sounding quite interested. He turned his head slightly, as if he was trying to point himself in the direction of the new voice.

"They were logging a new tract of land and . . . and . . ." Sue trailed off as she began sobbing.

Now that Sue had managed to get the ball rolling, Don was able to take over. "We were logging a new tract of land for a private individual. I dropped the crew off and went back to get the loader. When I came back they were gone, the road was gone, everything was gone. They had just disappeared. We haven't been able to reach them on the CB or on Mack's cell phone. The park service has been looking for them for the better part of a week now, but they haven't had the least bit of luck. Temple owns the land where I dropped them off at, but Temple has no record of any cutting taking place in the area. Sue did a little looking around on her own and found out you owned the land before Temple and we were wondering if you might know something about what's going on here."

Mr. Alford's eyes grew wide. "You're talking about that chunk of land off Highway Eighty-seven, between Fairmount and Six Mile?"

"Yes, sir."

"Oh, Jesus," Mr. Alford said. His breath became labored. He began sucking on his nosepiece so hard it caused his chest to rise and fall under the sheet. Don began to fear the old man was having a heart attack.

"You okay?" Don asked.

Mr. Alford nodded, but he continued to breathe into his machine for another couple of minutes before he spoke again.

"That . . . land is . . . cursed," Mr. Alford panted.

"What do you mean?" Sue asked with a sob. "What are you talking about?"

Mr. Alford held up a hand for them to wait a second. Keeping his mouth closed, he breathed deeply through his nose, getting as much oxygen as possible. His panting had slowed, but he was still breathing heavily.

"What do you mean cursed?" Don tried after several moments passed, but Mr. Alford only raised his hand again, and continued his labored breathing.

Close to five minutes passed in uneasy silence before Mr. Alford spoke again. When he finally began his explanation, his voice was slow and measured, in an attempt to keep from having to stop for oxygen. "That land is cursed by some sort of Indian Demon. My grandmother was full blood Cherokee Indian. She claimed we were descended from a long line of...oh, what the hell do you call them... medicine men, I guess. Anyway, she used to claim she could talk to the spirits and such. She told me that the land you're talking about is on a weak spot between this world and another. Weak spot, that's how she put it. You see, most of the time that land is just like the rest of the East Texas pineywoods, but every generation or so the demon in those woods gets hungry. It opens the gate and lets a few poor unsuspecting souls in. Her father, my great-grandfather, bought the land back in the late eighteen-hundreds—said it was our family duty to keep people from getting pulled in, because of our bloodline and all. I guess I didn't take the story as serious as I should have. I was offered cash for the land, and I sold it." Mr. Alford paused to take a long pull of oxygen.

"So you're saying they've slipped out of East Texas and straight into hell?" Don said, not believing a word he was hearing.

"No, I ain't talking about a Christian hell—hellfire, damnation, and some red goat-legged feller running around with a pitchfork," Mr. Alford replied.

"What then? What are you talking about?" Sue sobbed.

"It's like a door to a demon's home. My grandmother told me that a demon is a god in its own home."

"Okay," Don said, still not believing, "then what about the man who hired us? Was he some sort of demon in disguise?"

"God's got his preachers. What makes you think demons ain't got helpers in this world? The demon got hungry so he called on a helper to see that he got fed."

Don wasn't buying a word of what this old man was saying, but Sue was hanging on his every word. "How do they get out?" she asked, almost pleaded. "If they're in this demon's home, how do they get back here?"

Mr. Alford turned toward her, and this time it actually seemed as if his eyes were aimed right at her and maybe even a little focused. "I'm sorry, but there ain't no way out."

Sue began bawling uncontrollably, and Don found himself once again trying to console her. He hurried her out of the room and started walking her down the hall. His arm pulled tight around her shoulders, he repeatedly told her that the old man was crazy, that there wasn't an ounce of truth to his wild tale. However, in the back of Don's mind he began to realize that he would never see Mack, Roy, Harry, Eric, or Kevin again.

—Seventeen—

THE PREPARATIONS FOR this night's visit were made in grim silence. All the boys had to work with was the machete—it had been tucked into Kevin's belt when the barricade and the fire had disappeared—and there wasn't enough time for a trip to the vehicles to get equipment. In the few brief moments between twilight and darkness Kevin and Derek stood the bed up against the door—this would be their barricade for the night. Next, the boys broke the legs off the table, then used the machete to hack them into long wooden stakes. By the time these four makeshift weapons were finished darkness had fallen. Their faces were barely six inches apart as they braced their shoulders against the upended bed, listening for movement outside the door. They didn't have to wait long.

"I think I hear something," Derek whispered.

"I don't . . ." Kevin started, then he did hear it. Distant but heavy footfalls, several yards out, directly in front of the door.

The footfalls stopped.

Kevin and Derek looked into each other's eyes, their pulses racing. A bead of sweat trickled down the bridge of Derek's nose until the droplet hung precariously from the tip. The corners of Kevin's mouth began twitching nervously.

Suddenly the footfalls came again, this time in a rapid crescendo as the beast outside rushed straight for the door. There would be no circling the porch tonight.

The first blow was hard, knocking the bed away from the door and almost causing both boys to loose their footing. The weight of both the boys and the bed returned to the door, but no sooner had it slammed shut than another heavy blow was landed.

"Christ!" Derek swore between blows. "Let's just let it in and..." another blow knocked the boys back. They returned to their positions and Derek continued, "We can try to kill it!"

That desperate course of action had crossed Kevin's mind, but right now, feeling the power of the blows of that terrible creature, such an idea seemed like suicide. "No!" Kevin replied.

He had more to say, but the next blow cut him short. This time the bed was pushed so far back by the blow that the boys found themselves having to keep it from falling over on top of them rather than simply pushing it back into the door. Seeing that the door was now open a full two feet, Kevin, who was closest to the opening, forgot all about the bed and slammed himself into the door with everything he had. The door didn't even budge.

Derek let the bed fall to the floor and joined Kevin in an attempt to close the breach. Even with both of their weight, the door was continuing to open.

Derek turned so that his back was against the door and drew the machete from his belt. Kevin tried to take one of the two stakes from his belt, but a sudden jolt from the other side of the door caused him to lose his grip and drop one. Two of the other three stakes were now under the fallen bed. Kevin reached for his last stake.

Smoke and steam rose from the massive black hand as it reached around the door and grabbed Kevin by the left arm. The pain was excruciating. It felt as if his arm was on fire.

"It's got me!" Kevin shrieked, as the hand pulled him toward the opening.

Derek came around from his side of the door with the machete held high. He hacked down toward the exposed arm, but a quick tug brought Kevin closer to doorway, causing the missed blow to hit the door closer to Kevin's arm than the demon's.

Kevin instinctively grasped at the hand pulling him outside with his free hand, but when he touched the creature's wrist, the searing heat made him instantly release his grip.

Kevin was making another attempt to pull his stake from his belt when the demon gave a hard tug, bringing his head into contact with the edge of the door. Red and blue tracers flickered before his eyes. Kevin manage to get his weapon from his belt just as another tug slammed into the door once again, this time catching him with his head turned toward the door. Both of his lips were mashed bloodily against his teeth by the impact. The wooden stake fell to the floor.

Derek then jumped around Kevin and, standing directly in the opening in the doorway, swung at the hulking shape before him with everything he had.

His head swimming from the blows, Kevin could do little more than watch as Derek brought the rusty machete up and down in a valiant effort to save his life. Another tug on his arm once again caused a hard collision with the door. The room began to spin.

But the demon had loosened his grip, allowing Kevin to slump to the floor. The last sight he saw before slipping unconscious was the grim look on Derek's face as he flailed away at the creature standing in the doorway.

* * *

When Kevin came awoke the sun was out and he was alone.

The cabin was in perfect order. The bed in its proper place in the corner. Right above where Kevin lay sprawled on the floor, the table was set up neatly near the center of the room, with the paper, quill, and inkwell resting on the table's surface and the chair resting before it all. Everything was exactly as it was supposed to be, except Kevin—he hadn't been magically set right over night. His lips and nose throbbed and he didn't need a mirror to tell that more of his lower face was covered with dried blood than not. His left arm was severely burned, to the point that it was constantly oozing puss and blood.

Worst of all, Derek was gone. Apparently the demon had won the confrontation in the doorway, and, like the night Roy died, it had gone away satisfied with one kill.

Kevin pulled himself from under the table, then up into the chair. He ran his hand over his face, feeling the abrasions, lacerations, and swelling. He was a wreck.

He lifted himself painfully out of the chair and started toward the door, all for the fleeting hope that Derek would be outside waiting for him. Perhaps Derek would greet him on the porch with an exciting tale of how he had hacked the beast to death last night, and just now he had seen a helicopter circling overhead. But outside there was no Derek and no helicopter, just miles and miles of pine trees.

So many ancient pines standing proud in the morning sun should have made a sight fit for a painting, but there was something terribly wrong, something *unholy*, about all these trees without any other forms of life. No chattering mockingbirds, no barking squirrels, no early morning crickets, no noise whatsoever save that of the wind blowing through the trees. Born and bred in East Texas, Kevin never thought he'd see the day that he grew to despise the piney woods, but, then again, this wasn't East Texas. He was just now realizing how far from home he was.

He turned and walked back into the cabin and took a seat at the desk. He picked Brian Kinney's neatly stacked story up from the desk and flipped it over. He then removed the quill from the inkwell and began writing his tale. He wasn't sure how long it would take, but he had a feeling there would be enough time. In fact, he had a feeling darkness would fall at the very instant he laid his quill down, and, when that happened, he was going to step outside and meet his fate.

About the author

Byron Starr is the author of the nonfiction book *Finding Heroes*, the dark humor novel *Ace Hawkins and the Wrath of Santa Claus*, and the horror novel *Doppelganger*.

Byron lives in Hemphill, Texas.